'After I saw Jak[...] was pretty sure [...] father was. That's why I had [...] come and check.'

He quickly pulled her towards him and held her close. 'That photo is of my cousin, James. Jake is so like him as a boy that I was almost certain they were related. And that proves it.'

She gulped in an effort to stem the tears.

To give her time to come to terms with the enormity of the situation he flipped over the next couple of pages and uttered a gasp of amazement. One of the snaps there showed James holding a large canvas of a landscape. The truth slotted into place like the pieces of a jigsaw. He groaned. James was dead.

'I can hardly take it in, Tammy. How am I going to tell his mother he'll never come home...?' He gathered her gently into his arms and murmured, 'This is all so surreal...' He wiped the tears from her cheeks with his thumb and whispered, 'He was a lucky man to be so loved.'

'No, don't think that, Ben.' She sniffed. 'You've got it wrong...'

Although a Lancastrian by birth, **Sheila Danton** has now settled in the West Country with her husband. Her nursing career, which took her to many parts of England, left her with 'itchy feet' that she indulges by travelling both at home and abroad. She uses her trips to discover new settings for her books, and also to visit their three grown-up children, who have flown the nest in different directions.

Recent titles by the same author:

THE NURSE'S SECRET CHILD
ENDURING ATTRACTION
THE PATIENT LOVER
GOOD HUSBAND MATERIAL

A CHILD TO
CALL HIS OWN

BY
SHEILA DANTON

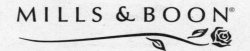

MILLS & BOON®

All the characters in this book have no existence outside the imagination of the author, and have no relation whatsoever to anyone bearing the same name or names. They are not even distantly inspired by any individual known or unknown to the author, and all the incidents are pure invention.

First published in Great Britain 2003
Harlequin Mills & Boon Limited,
Eton House, 18-24 Paradise Road, Richmond, Surrey TW9 1SR

© Sheila Danton 2003

ISBN 0 263 83477 8

Set in Times Roman 10½ on 11½ pt.
03-1003-49450

Printed and bound in Spain
by Litografía Rosés, S.A., Barcelona

CHAPTER ONE

'LOOKING for something?'

The resonant voice made Tammy jump. She swung round to discover a dark-haired man smiling down at her. 'You gave me a fright. I thought I was destined to solve this gigantic Space Invader game all by myself.'

Seven years' familiarity with the ancient hospital where she had trained had not prepared Tammy Penrose for finding her way around a brand-new hospital building created to outwit even Darth Vader.

He laughed. 'Your first day here. I can tell.'

'And silly me came without my laser-powered direction-finder.'

His dark eyes crinkled with amusement as he asked, 'Where are you heading?'

'The canteen.' His eyes were inviting her to laugh with him, but he was so breathtakingly impressive in his dark blue suit that all she could manage was to stumble out, 'Then back to Clarke Ward for the consultant's round.'

A flash of recognition crossed his face. 'You're Mike Rolf's new recruit?'

She nodded. 'Guilty as charged.'

'Welcome to the chest team.' His firm handshake triggered a shock wave that excited every nerve in her body. 'But as Mike's registrar, I can tell you we're going to have to hurry. So follow me.'

The effect of the contact between them was so overwhelming that it took her a couple of moments to realise that this was her immediate boss she'd been so flippant with. She retrieved her hand from his grasp and followed his lean and tightly muscled frame back the way she had come. When he led the way through one of the doors she had discounted as definitely not the canteen, she offered up a silent prayer of thanks that she would be working with someone so approachable. Not to mention his incredibly deep brown eyes and confident demeanour.

'Coffee?'

Dismissing her wandering thoughts, she nodded. 'Please.'

He handed over an empty mug. 'Help yourself from that machine.'

While she did and poured in a liberal amount of milk to cool it, he settled up with the cashier, then indicated an empty table.

'Thanks for this.' As she drank she got her first really good view of the man opposite and frowned slightly. 'I seem to know you from somewhere. Have our paths crossed before?'

He shook his head. 'I don't think so. Ben Davey. And you are?'

'Tamsin Penrose. Commonly known as Tammy.'

He was thoughtful as he extended a hand to her and held onto hers a fraction longer than she considered necessary. 'No, I'm sure our paths have never crossed, more's the pity.'

She looked up to find his dark eyes watching her through narrowed lids. His touch again sent an unaccustomed tremor skittering through her body and she wondered if he also sensed the stirring of mutual attraction between them.

Clearly not.

'Drink up. It's time to go.' He released her hand abruptly and quickly pushed his chair back, making it clear that, beyond finding his dogsbody for the next six months, he had no interest in her.

That suited her. Men were definitely off limits unless she

became a better judge of character, and, for her son's sake, completing her GP training as soon as possible was imperative. So for the foreseeable future relationships of any kind were out. She drained her mug and left the canteen behind her boss, keeping up with his long strides with difficulty.

'Mike tells me you qualified nearly three years ago, so are you intending to specialise in chest medicine?' He threw the query over his shoulder as he walked.

'I'm afraid not,' she gasped, as they arrived at the ward door to find her new consultant waiting.

Mike Rolf acknowledged them with a clipped smile. 'Good. You've met already. We can get the show under way at once.'

Having gathered at her interview with Mike Rolf that he would not tolerate fools gladly and didn't like to waste a moment, Tammy raised an eyebrow towards Ben in mute appeal.

'Sister Watson will have the notes trolley ready by the first bed,' he murmured quietly as the consultant marched into the ward. 'I'll do all the talking today.'

She flashed him a smile of thanks. Although she'd already been on duty for two and a half hours, Sister Watson hadn't allowed her a moment to discover what was going on with most of their patients. She had presented Tammy with a stack of request forms, some of which needed urgent blood samples. After that she had asked her to change two infusions sites and tidy up numerous other small jobs that had been neglected over the weekend.

'What's happening here?' The consultant had stopped at the bed of the first patient.

Tammy knew John Lowe had been admitted the previous Friday with a severe chest infection which was responding only slowly to the antibiotic being dripped in through a vein.

His was one of the two sets of notes she *had* read thoroughly before resiting his infusion.

Ben recited the details accurately and concisely.

'No culture results from the lab yet?' Mike frowned.

Ben shook his head. 'Afraid not. Could you get on to them as soon as we've finished, Tammy?'

She wrote a quick memo to herself while the consultant spoke to the patient, then listened to his chest. 'That doesn't sound too bad. Dr Davey tells me you're improving, albeit slowly. I think we'll leave things as they are until we know which bugs we're dealing with. Anything you want to ask?'

Mr Lowe shook his head.

'If you do think of anything, Dr Penrose and I will be around all day,' Ben told him with a gentle smile.

As they moved on round the ward and discussed the remainder of the patients, Tammy became increasingly impressed by both men. They wasted no time and yet gave each patient the impression that they had all the time in the world for them.

When the consultant left the ward, Ben led the way into the ward office and took the seat behind Sister Watson's desk.

Tammy, who was sorting through her notebook, sensed his dark eyes watching her pensively and felt a blaze of colour rise in her cheeks.

'Is something wrong?'

He hastily shook his head. 'I was just wondering why you've joined the chest team if you don't intend to specialise.'

'I hope to become a GP but so far have had no experience of what I expect to be a large part of my caseload.'

'Good thinking. The more you know about chests the fewer referrals you'll make, and that should make our life easier. At the moment we're asked to see many patients who could be treated at home.'

'You're hopeful if you think I'll learn enough in six months to make *that* much of a difference.'

He raised an amused eyebrow. 'I'll rise to that challenge and see that you do. Now, did you make a note of everything that's to be done today?'

Tammy nodded. 'I did. And I'd better start immediately. Goodness knows how I'll fit everything in.'

'We've been managing with locums until you arrived so I'm afraid you've got the weekend backlog to deal with as well as trying to find your way around a new system.'

'*And* a most confusing building,' she contributed ruefully.

'You'll soon get used to it. It's very easy once you know your way around. We could do with a few more door labels and signs, though. They are supposed to be on their way but I think they must be coming by the sea route.'

She laughed as she pulled the telephone towards her. 'I'll start with the lab results, I think.'

Ben nodded. 'I need to pop down to look at a chap in the admissions ward, and then I'll be back, hopefully, to give you a hand until it's time for the outpatient clinic this afternoon.'

'Outpatient clinic?' she groaned. 'Am I supposed to be there?'

'Not today. I think you've quite enough to do as it is. Bleep me if you find anything startling about John Lowe's bugs, won't you?'

She nodded and lifted a hand in farewell as her call was answered and she was already asking someone on the other end of the line for the results she needed.

Ben was as good as his word, and returned to the ward to take over a share of her duties. She was more than grateful when he started with updating the notes about the consultant's round.

Considering it was her first day, Tammy was surprised

how well they worked together. Ben appeared to know instinctively what she was thinking and did what needed to be done without disturbing her concentration on the task in hand.

Sneaking a furtive glance at his face as he pored over a set of notes, their eyes met as he did the same. She sensed in that moment that the attraction *had* been mutual earlier and felt a pang of regret that she hadn't met him before she'd met Jazz.

When midday approached, he came into the ward to find her completing X-ray request forms at the ward desk. 'When are you going to lunch?'

'Lunch? I'll give it a miss today. It won't do me any harm.'

He surveyed her carefully. 'I don't think I'd agree with that.'

'Believe me, it won't. Sister Watson has been plying me with food and drinks all morning.'

'Make sure you get something this evening, then. I warn you, the canteen closes pretty promptly. If you're not careful, you'll discover on Friday that you've not eaten all week.'

'No problem. I'll usually eat at home.'

'Ah. You've already found a place to live in Marton?'

'I didn't need to.'

She didn't elaborate and although Ben guessed it was because she was concentrating on the notes she was making, he couldn't resist asking, 'You're not living alone, then?'

'No.'

Again she didn't give details so, feeling snubbed, he said, 'I'll go and eat, then.'

Tammy nodded and then, looking up from her writing for the first time, she frowned. 'See you later.'

Making his way to the canteen, Ben groaned audibly as

Sister Watson joined him in the search for food. 'Aren't you well?'

'I think I've just put my foot in it with our new recruit.'

'Tut-tut. And her such a pretty little thing, too.' Jan Watson grinned. 'Did you make a pass at her?'

'Certainly not. I let my curiosity get the better of me.'

She laughed. 'You mean you tried to pry into her private life?'

He shrugged. 'I suppose you could call it that.'

Jan grinned knowingly. 'Threatened your immunity to the female sex, has she? I've always thought that would happen one day. I'm glad I'm here to witness it.'

Ben gave her a playful punch. 'It's nothing like that, and don't you start spreading rumours. I know what you're like.'

He knew the fact that he was apparently unattached had been a source of much speculative gossip when he'd first arrived at the hospital, and he didn't relish a repeat. Especially as there were no rings on Tammy's left hand. If his break-up with Deanna had taught him anything, it was to avoid career-women, especially if they were attractive.

He returned to the ward twenty minutes later, intending to ask Tammy if there was anything she needed to know before he went down to the outpatient clinic, but he couldn't find her and as Jan had returned a few minutes earlier, he didn't intend to ask.

However, it didn't stop her guessing why he was there. 'Taking a well-earned breather, if she's got any sense. I'll tell her you're missing her when she returns.'

'Don't you dare. You're a mischief-maker, Sister. You know where I am if I'm needed.'

Having rung her four-year-old son's nanny to check if all was well, Tammy returned to the ward. Jan came out of the office to greet her. 'You just missed Ben. He says he'll be in Outpatients if you need him.'

Her mind on what she needed to do next, Tammy nodded but made no comment.

'You'd be hard put to find a better consultant and registrar.'

Realising she was being rude, Tammy tried to look repentant. 'Sorry. I was miles away.'

'Problems?'

'What? No!' She laughed. 'I've just made a quick call to check all's well at home.' Sensing Jan was about to ask why it shouldn't be, she said, 'Now, in management-speak, I need to prioritise my outstanding tasks.'

'That'll never work in a hospital. Too many emergencies.'

Tammy grinned. 'I can but try.'

By the end of her shift on her first day on Mike Rolf's firm she was exhausted, but satisfied she'd left nothing urgent undone. On the way to the residency she took out her mobile phone and rang her nanny for the fourth time that day, and was relieved to hear there were no problems.

When she finally got to her on-call room, she flopped into her bed, too tired even to make herself a hot drink.

The ward staff, especially Jan Watson, had been wonderful. As well as keeping her blood-sugar levels topped up, they had given her as much help as they could.

She hadn't had a moment all day to think much about Ben Davey, but now his brooding features were filling her thoughts. Especially the watchful dark eyes that seemed to be searching for answers about her whenever they met. Technically she was on call that night, but he had left instructions that as it was her first day, he was to be called first if a need arose.

She was more than grateful for his consideration. She

hadn't come across many registrars willing to help their juniors out the way he had done. Had they met before? There was certainly something vaguely familiar about him, but his name meant nothing to her, so it could only have been a fleeting acquaintance. Whatever, she considered herself extremely lucky to be working with such a congenial team.

She was so tired she slept almost immediately.

In his room in the residency, which wasn't much larger than the on-call cells, Ben was reciprocating Tammy's thoughts. He had been instantly captivated by the features of the red-haired girl who had been frantically trying to find the canteen, and had wanted to help her.

To discover he would be working with her for the next six months was a bonus, especially when he discovered she had a sparkling sense of humour. Her vague feeling that they knew one another had puzzled him at the time and yet he knew there were only so many feature patterns in the world and quite often he could see a resemblance to someone he knew in a patient or member of staff.

His thoughts turned again to Tammy. Had she applied for the post because she already owned a house in Marton? And why should he be so interested? Reluctant to answer his own questions, he was just about asleep when the sound of his bleeper jarred him wide awake.

Tammy only woke when her bleeper had reached its loudest.

She fumbled for the bedside telephone and rang the number indicated.

'Dr Penrose.'

'I'm sorry to disturb you—'

'Who's this?'

'Staff Nurse Lennard, Doctor. I saw you before you went off duty.'

'What's the problem?'

'Dr Davey asked me to ring you.' Her voice carried a mixture of nervousness and apprehension.

'Is he already on the ward?'

'Yes. There's a big emergency. We need all the help we can get.'

Tammy sighed wearily. 'I'll be right there.'

When she walked into the ward corridor, Ben came to meet her. 'I'm sorry I had to wake you,' he whispered, 'but it's a general emergency call for all staff.' He slid an arm around her shoulder and guided her into the office.

'I'll tell you about it in here.' He closed the door so that he could talk in normal tones. 'I don't want to disturb the patients any sooner than necessary.'

She nodded then, conscious that he was still holding her, she moved to the side of the desk. 'What's happened?'

'You probably know Blacktrees Chemicals? Down by the river?'

She nodded. 'I should do. Half the men in town work there.'

'There's been an explosion. Don't know the cause or what chemicals were involved as yet.'

'How many were working in the area at the time?'

'Not so many as if it was the day shift. I understand the skeleton night shift is there just to keep the plant running.'

'That's something at least.'

'We're on first standby for the casualties. We may need extra beds.'

'We still have four empty?'

As he nodded, his bleeper shattered the silence that surrounded them. He clicked it off and snatched up the receiver. Tammy tried to work out what was happening from the few terse comments he made then, giving it up as hopeless, she walked to the chair on the other side of the office.

Almost immediately he grabbed her hand and pulled her out of it. 'Come on. Six just arrived in Casualty.'

When they arrived in the department, it was milling with professionals. It seemed every doctor and nurse who wasn't out of town had responded to the call and so far there weren't enough patients to keep them busy.

Tammy yawned widely.

Ben did the same and grinned. 'Don't. We'll have the whole department at it.' He was called into the first cubicle and Tammy sank onto the nearest chair.

'Where did such stunning beauty appear from at this time in the morning?' a smooth brown voice enquired.

'The residency,' she answered dryly.

'You work here?' The gangly owner of the voice whistled appreciatively. 'I don't believe it. When did you start?'

'Today—no, yesterday.'

'Doing what?'

'The same as you, I imagine.'

'And that is?'

'Medicine.'

Ben reappeared and she noticed a disparaging grin hovering over one corner of his lips. 'You're dealing with our resident stud well, Tammy. You've met your match here, Peter. She's obviously come across your type before.'

Peter pulled a long face. 'Just my luck, Ben. I might have known she'd be working for the only other unattached guy in the place.'

'I don't believe you're including yourself in that equation, Peter.' The mocking tone of his voice surprised Tammy, especially when he turned abruptly to her and said, 'Come and take a look at the chap in this cubicle.'

The patient had an oxygen mask over his nose and mouth and was lying back with his eyes closed.

The casualty officer attending him told them, 'Mr White—Robert—was in the yard when the explosion happened and was thrown to the ground.'

'Chemical exposure?'

'The paramedic doesn't think so.'

Ben nodded and asked the patient, 'Have you had any chest problems before?'

Rob White didn't hear the question, but when it had been repeated slowly he shook his head.

Ben took out his stethoscope and after carrying out a thorough examination of the patient's chest, back and front, he listened carefully to the breath sounds.

'What's he like without the oxygen?'

'The paramedic said he was gasping for breath.'

Ben checked the information displayed on the monitor screen and asked, 'Have you coughed up any blood?'

Rob White again had difficulty hearing the question but when he did he shook his head.

After another careful examination of the patient, Ben said, 'We'll get a chest X-ray. And could you check his ears, Tammy? The blast has probably perforated one, or both of his eardrums. Give me a shout if you're worried.'

With the help of one of the nursing staff, Tammy organised the X-ray and found an otoscope to check the patient's ears. She discovered his left one had indeed perforated, but the right one seemed OK.

She searched out Ben and handed him the X-ray he'd ordered, and in answer to the query posed in his raised eyebrows she shook her head.

'Nothing obvious at the moment,' he agreed, 'but problems could develop over the next forty-eight hours so we need to admit him and keep a close eye on him.'

He slipped an arm along her shoulder and turned her towards the patient. 'OK if I leave it to you to tell him?'

Tammy nodded as Ben scribbled on the patient's chart. 'What about painkillers?'

'I've written them up and we'll get the ear, nose and throat boys up to see that damaged eardrum tomorrow.'

Tammy made the necessary arrangements and was about to leave the emergency department with her charge when Ben came in search of her. 'Tell them there's another for admission. This chap was exposed to a cocktail of chemicals—he's showing symptoms of asthma so far, but we don't know yet exactly what chemicals were involved.'

'Surely he does.'

'He's told us those he can remember, but the exact records have been destroyed.'

'I see. Looks like we're off, Ben. I'll be on the ward if you need me.' She followed Rob White's trolley to the lift.

He was just about settled when the patient Ben had warned her about arrived. He was accompanied by one of the emergency nurses who told her, 'Percy Good for you.'

Tammy helped to transfer him to the bed nearest to the office and linked him up to the bedside monitor and the piped oxygen supply.

'I'll leave you in Dr Penrose's capable hands now, Percy.' The nurse smiled at Tammy. 'And the doctor you met in Casualty will be up shortly.' She handed over the record card and moved out of the patient's hearing. 'Ben wants you to keep a close eye on him. This is what we've done so far.'

Tammy scanned the details and nodded. 'OK. What's happening down there?'

'Not a lot. Most of the other casualties are being transferred to the burns unit and it seems there are far fewer than expected.'

'Thank goodness for that.'

'Hopefully we'll be standing down soon and can get back to bed.'

Tammy laughed ruefully. 'Not me. I'm on call tonight.'

'Tough luck. But I'm sure working with the delectable Dr Davey will make up for it. That's if you can manage to divert his attention from his patients for even a moment. The rest of us haven't discovered the secret as yet.'

Tammy could hear her chortling at her own wit as she made her way down the corridor, and though she was momentarily irritated she dismissed all thought of it as she went to take a look at her two admissions.

Rob White was sleeping peacefully, so she checked the monitor readings. Satisfied, she moved on to take a closer look at Percy Good.

He was moving restlessly and tugging at the tube supplying him with oxygen.

'Is that bothering you?' she asked him quietly.

'Not really, but why do I need it?'

'It's to help your breathing.'

He pulled at the lines leading to the monitor.

'What are these for?'

'They help us to check how you're doing without waking you.'

He gave a slight nod. 'How am I doing?'

'Very well, so why don't you try and get some sleep? I'll be here.'

'All night?'

'What's left of it.'

He closed his eyes and soon drifted off into a light doze. Tammy settled on the chair beside him and noted the monitor readings down on his chart.

She'd just finished when Ben appeared. He took a look at both patients then indicated with his head that they should move into the office.

He sat down behind the desk and yawned. 'Look promising?'

She nodded. 'Let's hope they stay that way. How are the rest of the casualties?'

'They've all been transferred to the burns unit. They were the ones closest to the explosion.'

'Do we know what caused it yet?'

He shook his head. 'Nor exactly what chemicals were awaiting disposal, and they seem to be the ones involved. Hopefully daylight will change that.'

Tammy checked her watch. 'Like now. It's nearly six.'

'Thank goodness that wasn't as bad as it could have been. Let's adjourn to the canteen. I could do with some breakfast and then a spot of shut-eye.' He rested his hand lightly on the small of her back. 'I'm sorry I had to disturb you, Tammy.'

'I *was* officially on call.'

'Maybe, but two nights running when you've only just started here is not on.'

Tammy had been so busy the previous day that she hadn't really registered that she was on call for successive nights. She lifted a resigned eyebrow and shrugged. 'I've coped before.'

'I'm sure you have, but we *are* supposed to be getting better in that respect. Mind you, when it's an emergency call to all staff, as it was earlier, I'd have had to contact you at home anyway.'

'I'll try and get through the routine work as quickly as possible and perhaps have a short nap later.'

'I'll help.'

She looked at him in amazement. 'Certainly not. I at least had the luxury of four hours' sleep last night.'

Ben grinned. 'I managed nearly an hour.'

He pushed open the door of the canteen and waited for Tammy to go in before following her to join a larger number of bleary-eyed staff members than were usually to be found at breakfast in any hospital.

The cook gave them an apologetic smile. 'If you want something cooked it'll be some time. Wasn't expecting this rush.'

Ben smiled. 'We'll have coffee while we wait.'

'Full breakfast for both?'

He nodded, then turned to Tammy and queried, 'That is all right, is it?'

'It's more than all right. I'm starving.'

'You didn't remember to get to the canteen on time last night?'

'How did you guess?'

'So you had nothing all day?'

'Jan and her staff kept me fed and watered.'

He shook his head despairingly. 'You can't survive these long hours on snacks!'

'I don't intend to.' She laughed. 'I enjoy my food far too much.'

They carried their coffee over to a corner table and when they were settled he asked, 'What made you come *here* to learn about chests—were you attracted by the new building?'

'Not really. After St Mungo's anything would be better. Was that what brought you here?'

He shook his head. 'I worked with Mike when I was a senior houseman and he was a senior registrar. When he was setting up this new department, he suggested I join him. I liked the thought of working in a new hospital from its first day and we do work well together.'

'I can see that.'

'So what *did* make you choose Marton?'

'I am on a recognised GP scheme, but for personal reasons I wanted to work out my own placements. I thought this would be a great opportunity so I wrote and asked for either a medical or children's placement here.'

'Sensible, I suppose, when you already have a home in Marton.'

Despite his words, Tammy thought her reasons didn't seem to meet with his approval so she quickly explained. 'I was brought up here.'

'Ah. I see.' He seemed happier with that. 'You live with your parents.'

It was a statement rather than a question and she hastened to correct his incorrect assumption. 'Actually, I don't. I have my own place.'

His animation was short-lived and she frowned as he went on to ask, 'You trained at St Mungo's?'

She nodded.

'Did you remain there once you were qualified?'

She shook her head. 'I moved around some of their satellite hospitals. Why?'

'Idle curiosity I suppose you could call it. It usually helps with the working relationship to know something about one another's backgrounds.'

'Where did *you* train?'

'St Luke's.' Their breakfast arrived as he spoke and Ben leapt from his chair to collect cutlery and condiments. On his return he appeared to have forgotten the thread of their conversation and started talking about the patients.

'Mr Lowe seems to be responding OK, doesn't he?'

She nodded. 'I took a look at him just before coming down here. He seems much better today.'

'There's a drug company presentation about chest infections on Monday evening. Fancy coming to hear what they have to say?'

'That sounds interesting. Can I let you know on the day?' She checked the page in her diary. 'Nothing down for that evening, but I'll need to check if I'm on call or not. And if I'm swamped with work I'd rather catch up here.'

He rested his hands on her shoulders so that she couldn't

escape his intent gaze and said quietly, 'Even though they're putting on a buffet supper for us?'

She laughed nervously. 'Now you're tempting me.'

'Good. I meant to. You know what they say?'

After the casualty nurse's comment about Ben, she hated to think what was already being said about her. She felt her cheeks start to colour, and answered apprehensively, 'I can't imagine…'

'Don't worry, I'm not repeating gossip. Just an old saw with a lot of truth in it. ''All work and no play makes Jill a dull girl.'''

Momentarily relieved, she smiled. 'Thanks for the compliment.'

'Hey, I didn't mean to imply you were dull. I just want to stop you heading that way.'

'You're so kind, sir.' She tugged at an unruly strand of hair that was threatening to cover one eye, but even as she spoke she was trying to work out what her colleagues had said about her that made him recognise immediately the reason for her embarrassment.

She was plucking up her courage to ask when a shadow fell across the table and she looked up to see Peter standing there. 'Can I join you?'

'You can have my chair. I'm going to get my head down.' She was surprised by Ben's obvious irritation as he stacked his dirty dishes together and nodded to Tammy. 'See you later.'

'Now, that's what I call extreme gallantry in the face of competition.' Peter either hadn't noticed Ben's manner or had ignored it, and attacked his eggs and bacon with relish.

Tammy frowned. Remembering Ben's description of the man opposite, she said, 'I'm afraid I won't be staying long. Too much to do, I'm afraid.'

'You mean that chauvinist has gone to bed, leaving you to do all the work. Shame on the man.'

Aware that his extravagant remarks were nothing more than a game, Tammy knew she could easily handle him. 'That's the last thing I'd call him. He took my calls last night until the general emergency arose.'

'Did he?' He assumed a rueful look 'Alas, I can't compete. I like my sleep too much.'

'I wasn't properly introduced earlier. You are?'

'Dr Govan, dermatology registrar, at your service. But call me Pete.'

Tammy burst out laughing. 'I should have known. You don't have many nights disturbed by emergencies.'

'Why do you think I chose skin as my speciality? I want a social life.'

'And you think the rest of us don't? I've enjoyed our chat this morning, Dr Govan, but I'm afraid some people *do* have emergencies so I have to go.'

'Call me Pete. Please,' he pleaded, grasping her hand. 'I'll count the minutes to our next chat.'

She found her way back to Clarke Ward with a cynical smile on her face, which soon faded when she found Ben in the office, watching her with narrowed eyes. 'I thought you'd gone to bed.'

'I wanted to check the two admissions first.'

'How are they doing?'

'Both stable. I'm hopeful that we won't have any further problems with either of them, but it's early days yet. Percy's breathing isn't improving and he asked if I thought his lungs would be permanently damaged.'

'I think he's quite a worrier. About everything.'

'Mmm. I get that impression as well, but I suppose it's not surprising after what happened.'

'Thanks for doing my calls last night and thanks for breakfast. I owe you.'

'My pleasure.'

He smiled briefly, but his manner had changed since he'd

left the canteen. Perhaps he didn't like Peter. Tammy shrugged. Not surprising really. Ben seemed too dedicated to his work to appreciate his colleague's flirtatious attitude. She shrugged. As far as she could see, there was no harm in Pete. Perhaps Ben should apply his maxim to himself—'all work and no play makes Jack a dull boy.'

CHAPTER TWO

AFTER two nights on call, Tammy was more than ready to leave on Wednesday evening the moment she had handed over to the covering house officer.

She groaned when Ben came into the office just as she picked up her car keys.

'I'm not welcome. I can tell.'

'Too true. I'm off home, unless you're about to say I'm needed.'

'No way. There's nothing that can't wait until tomorrow.'

'Thank goodness for that. I seem to have been here for a lifetime.'

'Not surprising. It's two whole days and nights since I found you wandering the corridors.'

'At least in that time I've learnt my way around.'

'Phew!' She grinned as he feigned relief with a swipe of his brow before saying, 'Get off home now, before I do find you something. And, Tammy?'

'Yes?'

'You've done well. It's good to have you on the team.'

She made her way out to the car park, warmed by his appreciation and thinking, not for the first time, how lucky she was to have him as a registrar. He seemed to be everything Jazz had never been. Caring, considerate… Don't even go there, she warned herself. You need to concentrate on Jake and your career. You're a bad judge of character. Remember?

Jake flung himself at her as she opened the front door. 'Mummy, Mummy, Mummy,' he squealed.

She gathered him in her arms as he swung himself off the floor with his arms around her neck. 'Hello, love. What a welcome.' Over his shoulder she smiled at Lauren and asked, 'Everything OK?'

'We're fine, aren't we, Jake?'

He was too busy dragging his mother to the playroom to answer.

Laughing, Tammy asked, 'Have you plans for your free evening, Lauren?'

'Marcus is picking me up later.'

'Marcus?'

'That new chap I met last week. I might be late back.'

'No problem as long as you're there for me to leave at the usual time in the morning.'

Tammy turned her attention to Jake for the rest of the evening, and after more than enough bedtime stories to make up for the nights she'd been absent, he eventually fell asleep. Not long afterwards Tammy made her own way to bed to catch up on her lost sleep—a move she was glad she'd made when Jake snuggled in beside her extra early the next morning, clutching more books to be read.

As on the previous evening, every book was about the tank engine, Thomas, and his friends.

'This red one is James. And the green one Percy,' he told her excitedly. 'Can we go and see Thomas? On Saturday?'

Tammy knew the local preserved railway ran 'Thomas' days, but only once or twice a year.

'He's a very busy engine, but if I hear he's going to stop at Marton, you can see him, I promise. If I'm working, Lauren will take you.'

He stuck out his bottom lip. 'Want to go with you.'

Tammy felt a sudden rush of tears pricking at her eyes. She'd love to spend more time with him, and once she moved into general practice she'd make sure she did. In the meantime, she had this weekend free and would make the most of every moment with him.

Tammy sat in on the outpatient clinic for the first time the following Monday and so was still catching up on the ward work when Ben joined her in the office a couple of hours after the clinic had ended. 'Are you sufficiently up to date here to come to that drug presentation I mentioned?'

'I think so, but could we just go through these reports?'

'Sure.'

'There are one or two I'm not sure about—like this one. Some of these results seem to be slightly out of the normal limits.'

He rested a hand on her shoulder as he took the pathology forms and perused the figures on them for a few seconds before reassuring her. 'Taking into account the drugs we're giving him, these are acceptable.'

'That's what I thought, but—'

'I'd much rather you check than be sorry.' His smile of approval lit up his dark eyes, making Tammy acutely conscious of his proximity.

Too conscious. She quickly slid from beneath his hand and turned to face him. 'Are we going to let Percy out soon? He's fretting about his job.'

'I should think that's the last thing he needs to worry about. His employers will probably be only too keen to keep him happy in case he looks for compensation.' His eyes raked over her face as he spoke and she guessed he was surprised by her sudden move.

'Does that mean you think he's likely to have problems with his chest from now on?'

'Not necessarily, but he's worked at Blacktrees since he was a lad, and over the years has been exposed to a variety of chemicals. Apparently there wasn't much protection available, especially in the early days, so he could have had a weakness there already.'

'What about checking his GP records?'

'Apparently Percy is one of the old school and wouldn't have any truck with doctors, whether it's his GP or the one who held a clinic at the factory.'

'That's odd when you consider what an anxious man he is.'

'Not really. He doesn't trust them. He doesn't trust us. That's why he questions everything we do. I'd like to bet he doesn't trust banks with his money either.'

'Unusual in someone of his age.'

'Probably his late mother's influence. He never married and has never moved from the family home, has he? And probably doesn't mix socially with the men he works with either.'

'He's certainly had no visitors that I know of. Apart from the official ones asking questions.'

'There've been a good few of those but they still don't seem able to discover the cause.'

'As no one was killed I don't think there is the urgency to find out. Apparently inspectors are too thin on the ground.'

'Who told you that? The inspectors themselves?'

'How did you guess?'

He grinned and tapped the side of his nose. 'Inside information. I had a long chat with Rob White before he was discharged.'

'And?'

'He hinted that health and safety wasn't a priority at Blacktrees.'

'Hopefully that explosion will have taught the management a lesson.'

'Maybe. If they don't get away with it. But if there aren't enough inspectors...' He shook his head, then shrugged.

'Hopefully there will be a proper inquiry. Still, that's not our problem tonight. Getting to that buffet while there's still some food is. Now, what else is there that can't be left? Time's getting on.'

She'd been about to ask what they could do about it but, sensing his impatience, she suppressed her indignation on behalf of the chemical workers and sorted through the remainder of the reports and quickly extracted those she still wasn't sure about.

They worked steadily for another half-hour, but Ben's mind wasn't completely focussed on his work. He found Tammy's presence distracting and when they eventually made their way to his car, he couldn't resist trying to find out more about her private life, albeit not directly. 'I hope I'm not spoiling any plans you had for this evening.'

She shook her head. 'I'd nothing planned. If I had I wouldn't be here. I'm not in the habit of cancelling arrangements for something more—or less—attractive.'

He sighed. Why was she still so careful not to give anything away? Or did she just not like idle chatter? Even that practised interrogator, Jan Watson, seemed to have found out little about her.

'Am I spoiling someone else's evening, then?'

'I doubt it.'

Trying to hide his curiosity, he shrugged and said, 'I see.'

'I don't expect you do. I live with my four-year-old son. And he's hopefully in the land of Nod by this time.'

'Son?' he echoed, surprised to find his heart plummeting with disappointment. 'You have a four-year-old son? How on earth do you manage to work such long hours?'

'A wonderful nanny.'

He inclined his head. 'Expensive. Is his father a doctor as well?'

'His father is dead. Jake is, no doubt, in bed by this time and the nanny ensconced in the living room in the arms of her current boyfriend. Now do you understand why I won't be missed?'

Taken aback by her stark statement, Ben sensed she didn't intend to discuss the matter further, but her face was so bleak that he wanted to take her in his arms and comfort her, but he guessed it wouldn't be welcome.

Instead, he squeezed her nearest hand and asked gently, 'Would you like something more substantial than the drug company will provide?'

She shook her head. 'The buffet is fine by me. What about you?'

'I had lunch. You didn't.'

'Are you checking up on me?' The laugh that accompanied her query appeared forced and Ben wondered if she felt he was monitoring her every movement.

Which he supposed he was—because she intrigued and attracted him. Deciding it would be better to make a joke of his answer, he grinned. 'Definitely. I need to know you have enough energy for all the work I intend to load you with.'

'No problem there! I love food but I prefer my own cooking to what the canteen has to offer. When I'm on call I'll try to bring something in with me.'

'Buffet it is, then.' He continued the journey in silence, aware that on the subject of her private life he was going to have to tread very carefully.

Tammy was grateful for the silence. It gave her the opportunity to get her emotions under control. She'd known she couldn't keep her son a secret, but she hated the well-meant sympathy that always accompanied her admission difficult to cope with. She didn't need it. It had been almost a relief when Jazz had been killed. Not that she would have wished anything so awful to happen to him, but his death had made things so much easier for her.

But that was something she could never share. Not even

with her parents. In case it got back to Jake. She was determined he would never know the truth about his father. It was her secret and that was the way it must remain, however much she longed to shock some people by telling the truth when they sniffily asked why she and Jazz had never married.

She was grateful that Ben hadn't uttered meaningless words of compassion as most other people did. It made them feel better for having broached the subject, but it always made her feel much worse. She supposed it was because Ben was a doctor that he must have recognised immediately that she wasn't telling him everything and that to offer suffocating sympathy was not appropriate.

She stole a glance at his face and was mortified to find him doing the same. He gave her a warm smile and hurriedly returned his eyes to the road, leaving her only too aware of the unspoken affinity she sensed always there between them.

When he eventually spoke, he turned to the safer subject of medicine. 'How much do you know about the treatment of chest infections?'

'Not much more than I learnt at medical school. Were you thinking about bronchitis? Pneumonia? Or—'

'Start with bronchitis.'

'If the patient is usually healthy it is more often than not viral so we'd be unlikely to see it in hospital.'

'What would lead you to suspect it might be bacterial?'

'If it hasn't cleared with TLC and time. Or if the patient has chronic bronchitis or obstructive airways disease.'

'You'd recommend antibiotic treatment for those cases?'

'Yes, tailored to the specific bug as soon as a culture result is available.'

He nodded. 'And if they are smokers?'

'It doesn't help, so try to persuade them to give up.'

'What about pneumonia?'

'In adults? More often than not it's bacterial.'

He nodded. 'Right again. OK, we're here.'

'Thank goodness for that. I know I said I wanted to learn as much as I could about chests but you had me worried for a moment.'

Ben was relieved to see she was laughing. He'd been so anxious to avoid making her obvious uneasiness worse that he'd gone over the top with his questioning.

'Sorry about that. I was just trying to discover how much chest medicine you'd done in the past.'

'I *was* beginning to wonder if I'd made some appalling mistake in the last week.'

'Certainly not,' he reassured her. 'I've been very impressed with your work so far.'

As they'd arrived at the presentation venue, Tammy didn't bother to answer, but nevertheless a surge of satisfaction spread through her veins. This warmth brought an increased colour to her cheeks as Ben was ribbed by several of the other doctors there, who all seemed to know him.

'Feeding your girlfriend on the drug rep's budget, are you, Ben?'

'Getting tight in your old age?'

Ben laughed and took it all in his stride, and introduced Tammy when he got a chance to speak. 'This is my new assistant. She's a GP trainee.'

They all nodded a greeting and one clapped Ben on the back and told him, 'I might have known. You always did know how to pick 'em.'

'I had absolutely nothing to do with her selection. I didn't meet Tammy until her first day with us. Now, let's get to this food. We're starving.'

As they made their way towards a side room with food-laden tables, he took her arm and said quietly, 'This isn't turning out to be a very pleasant evening for you, is it? But I can assure you they don't mean any harm.'

She shrugged. 'Looking round the room, I guess I'm a novelty. It's more like a men's club.'

He laughed. 'I'm afraid there is usually a greater pre-ponderance of males. I guess that's because...' He hesi-tated.

'Yes?' she enquired innocently, although well aware of what he'd been about to say.

'Well...' Realising he was in danger of giving her the impression he was prejudiced, he hesitated before deciding how to word his reply. 'If you didn't have a nanny you'd have to be at home with your son this evening, wouldn't you?'

'You're saying that, despite female doctors making up half of the workforce, chauvinism still exists in the medical profession!'

He nodded ruefully. 'I guess that is what I'm saying.' He rushed on to say, 'But I assure you I don't subscribe to it.'

She grinned. 'It doesn't make any difference to me whether you do or don't.' She handed him a plate. 'I'm more interested in the food.'

'Me, too.'

They filled their plates and made their way to the far corner of the room where there were a couple of seats.

'I'll get some drinks. What's your tipple?'

'Red wine.'

'Of course. Just what the doctor ordered.' He grinned and placed his plate on his chair. 'Back in a moment.'

When he eventually returned, she had cleared her plate and was talking to a middle-aged doctor who had taken the seat on the other side of her.

'Hello, Ben,' he said, greeting the arrival of the wine with approval. 'Is that for me?'

'Certainly not. You can scrimmage for your own. This glass is for my new colleague. Have you been introduced?'

They both shook their heads.

'Tammy, let me introduce Rees Jones, consultant in communicable diseases at Marton General. Rees, this is Tamsin Penrose.'

He nodded his acknowledgement and she asked, 'I suppose you have to deal with some multi-drug-resistant infections suffered by AIDS sufferers?'

'I do, but that's not why I'm here.'

'Like us, you're here for the food, aren't you, Rees?'

'Not wholly. My interest is in the new tuberculosis regimes.'

'TB?' Tammy raised a rueful eyebrow. 'That's something I've not come across as yet.'

'You will in general practice,' Ben told her. 'It's on the increase. Quite rapidly, too.'

'There've been a few articles about that recently, haven't there?' She raised a rueful eyebrow.

Whilst Ben was driving Tammy back to the hospital to pick up her own car, he couldn't resist trying to find out just a little bit more about her. 'It's not common knowledge at the hospital that you have a son, is it?'

'No. I don't exactly hide it, but I don't broadcast it either. I'm always afraid I'll be accused of neglecting my work because I want to get home to him.'

'You sound as if that's happened to you in the past.'

She nodded. 'Prejudice does exist, especially when people realise I'm a single mother.'

'Has it ever occurred to you that fathers might also like to get home to see their children?'

She thought he sounded wistful and, watching him closely, asked hesitantly, 'You're talking personally?'

'I'm afraid not.' The words were uttered vehemently and, remembering Peter had hinted Ben was unattached when he'd said she was working for the only other available guy in the hospital, Tammy was puzzled. But as the only gossip she'd heard about him had been the casualty nurse hinting his work was the only thing important to him, perhaps his family was some distance away.

'I hear you're looking for somewhere else to live. Have you had any luck?'

Ben shook his head. 'But I can't really claim to have been trying very hard.'

She swung round and gave him a surprised look. 'Why's that? Are you thinking of making another career move?'

'Nothing like that. Not at the moment anyway. But house-hunting is time-consuming. And I've just been too busy.'

'So where's your home at the moment?'

He hesitated. 'Er, that's hard to say. I don't have one. Not really.'

'You don't have one?' That knocked her earlier theory on the head. 'And you haven't seen anything at all that takes your fancy in Marton?'

'Oh, yes. There've been one or two but they haven't worked out.'

She nodded sympathetically. 'If you're not on the spot at the right time, you lose them in this seller's market, don't you?'

'I guess so, but I haven't got that far. They just haven't been right.'

Tammy frowned and couldn't resist prompting him to reveal more. 'I expect you're after a biggish house?'

'Not necessarily.' He turned his attention to a difficult junction, leaving Tammy to wonder even more about him.

When they arrived back in the hospital car park, she took out her keys and said, 'Thanks for a pleasant evening. It's been helpful.'

'Come in for a cup of coffee and we can consolidate on what you've learnt.'

'I won't tonight, thanks, Ben. Some other time perhaps.'

He looked disappointed but immediately asked, 'What about a meal later in the week, then?'

'Sounds nice, but I'm not sure…'

'We don't have to settle on a day now. Probably easier with the on-call rotas in front of us anyway.'

She nodded, relieved not to have to make a decision until she could get her chaotic thoughts into some sort of order. She couldn't deny that, against her better judgement, she had been tempted. But her relationship with Jazz had left her wary of involvement with any man. At least until she knew where they were coming from.

The next few days sped by in a constant struggle to find a sufficient number of beds for the emergencies being admitted so, after insisting that he would be able to manage on his own, Percy was allowed to escape on Wednesday morning. As he packed up his meagre belongings Tammy asked, 'Is there someone who can collect you?'

'No.'

'I'll try and organise some transport, then, but you may have to wait.'

'I'll be all right on me own,' he muttered.

'I know you feel fine walking around the ward, but it'll be a different matter when the fresh air hits you.'

'I tried it already. Yesterday. I'll get home easy.'

'You live alone, don't you? You'll need food.'

'Corner shop has all I want.'

Tammy sighed. She knew that once he'd made up his mind there would be no changing it. She returned to the office and found Ben there. 'Percy is determined to get himself home. I told him about official transport but he's not prepared to wait.'

'All organised. The personnel manager from the factory is on his way.'

Tammy looked at him suspiciously. 'That's unusual, surely.'

'Not if they're running scared.'

She frowned. 'What are you trying to say?'

'They know Percy will soon forget the accident happened if they keep him happy.'

'Is that a good thing?'

He shrugged. 'It is for them. That's why the personnel manager is willing to put himself out.'

'They were doing something illegal, then?'

'I certainly wouldn't say that but I think it's pretty clear they weren't exactly conforming to regulations.'

'So that's the reason for all the official visits?'

'No. They'd have happened anyway.'

'So why…?'

'Perhaps I'm just a cynic, but when no one can tell us what chemicals were involved in the explosion and what workers like Percy might have been exposed to in the past, it set me thinking.'

'Go on,' she joshed. 'The last thing I would have put you down as is a cynic.'

'That's because you don't know me very well.'

Too true. Since Monday she'd being thinking exactly that herself. 'I suppose our training makes us that way.' She settled at the desk to write a discharge note for Percy to take to his GP. 'So I won't be surprised if this never reaches the health centre.'

She saw Ben watching with amusement when Percy pushed it into his back pocket. 'I can't emphasise too strongly how important it is that your doctor sees this. It details the drugs we want him to continue prescribing for you.' Percy nodded, but she could see he wasn't listening. 'Now, you won't forget, will you?'

He shook his head and lifted the plastic carrier bag containing his meagre belongings. 'I'll be off now.'

'If you wait a few minutes, I understand someone from Blacktrees is on the way to collect you.'

'If that's right, I'd best sit myself down here for a minute.'

Tammy noticed the relief on his face as he took the weight from his feet and guessed he wasn't feeling quite as well as he'd been making out.

She could only spare a few moments to talk to the man who collected Percy but to Tammy he seemed genuinely interested in his employee's welfare and he promised to keep an eye on Percy and see the letter reached its destination safely.

She intended to tell Ben she thought he'd got it wrong, but for the next couple of days emergency followed emergency, leaving her barely time to draw breath. So, apart from the occasional discussion about a patient, it was late on Friday afternoon before she spoke to Ben for any length of time.

He arrived in answer to her bleep.

'Sister Burns on the admissions ward has two patients needing beds and there's only one available. The bed co-ordinator wants to know if there's anyone fit enough for discharge, but I don't think so.'

Ben ran his finger down the list of patients and shook his head. 'All I can offer is to transfer the fittest to a ''sleeper'' bed elsewhere in the hospital so that we can keep an eye on him. The co-ordinator will have to find us one for a night or two.'

'''Sleeper'' bed?' she frowned.

'Not what it sounds like, Tammy. Unfortunately.' He grinned suggestively, making colour flood to her cheeks. 'It's an empty bed on another ward. Mr Lowe is about the fittest but he's certainly not well enough to go home. I'll get on to Jan Watson and she can arrange it.'

Struggling to avoid his searching gaze, she asked, 'Does this happen often?'

Ben nodded as he wrote in John Lowe's notes.

'But it's a new hospital.'

'The trust could only afford to replace the same number of beds as were in the old hospital.'

'What a wasted opportunity.'

He shrugged. 'Maybe, but who'd look after them? It's all we and the nursing staff can do to cope with the numbers we've got.'

'I suppose you're right.'

He crossed the room and laid a forefinger lightly on her arm. 'I know I am. You—' he reinforced the word with a light tap '—and I were going to arrange an evening out, but we haven't even had chance to do that.'

Only too conscious of the needle heat his touch aroused within her, she told him quickly, 'It'll have to be next week at least. I'm on call all weekend.'

'So you won't see your son at all?'

Overwhelmed by his sympathetic tone, she hesitated before answering, 'Probably not, although if there is a lull at any time, and only if, Lauren, the nanny, or my mother will bring him to visit me in my room.'

He shook his head. 'Sadly, I think that could be a forlorn hope.'

She nodded her agreement but to avoid his searching gaze she started to flick through a set of notes. 'Mum and Dad'll make it up to him.'

'They keep in touch?' He removed the notes from her reach, and she could do nothing but look up at him as she answered, 'They're both out at work during the week, so if I'm working weekends they take the opportunity to spoil him and give Lauren a break.'

'But you wouldn't move in with them?'

'I've been independent too long for that.' She sought to

escape the intimacy she sensed developing. 'It would spell disaster. And talking of disasters, I must go and check Mr Wilbur.'

He sighed and said, 'That's the chap with obstructive airways disease who came in yesterday, isn't it?'

She nodded. 'He seems to be slowly responding to the intravenous antibiotics, but it's early days yet. He seems to have had one crisis with his health after another recently.'

Ben nodded thoughtfully. 'I'll come with you. I was reading through his notes earlier and wondered if there's something he's not telling us.'

She frowned. 'Like what?'

'Problems at home? Started smoking again?' He shrugged. 'It's difficult to know unless he's willing to confide in us.'

On their way into the ward he spoke to Jan about the bed problem and left it in her hands.

As they pulled the curtains round Mr Wilbur's bed to take a look at him, his monitor sounded a loud warning and the patient clutched at his chest.

'Hell. He's arresting,' Ben said.

Tammy pushed the cardiac arrest button to call for help before struggling to remove the head of the bed.

Ben helped her and then started manual cardiac resuscitation until the crash team arrived.

Within minutes the bed was surrounded by staff and equipment.

Ben and Tammy assisted where and when they were needed. When the patient's condition had been stabilised, the anaesthetist in charge told them, 'We'll move him to Intensive Care for the night. I can keep a closer watch on him there.'

The anaesthetist and his team remained to assist the porters in moving the patient to ITU. Ben and Tammy helped with all the paraphernalia that accompanied him, then,

when he had been transferred, brought the empty one back
to the ward.

'Problem solved,' Ben said, slinging an arm around
Tammy as they made their way out of the ward. 'That was
hairy for a few moments. But you did well.'

'Do you think he'll be back tomorrow?'

'I doubt it. Poor chap had enough problems to contend
with without suffering a heart attack.'

They were both thoughtful as they made their way into
the empty office.

'Are—?'

'Do—?'

They both spoke at once then stopped, so Tammy said,
'You first.'

'I was going to ask if you thought you'd cope OK this
weekend.'

'I should hope so. There's always your opposite number
if I need advice.'

Ben nodded. 'I suppose so. It's a pity I've arranged to
be away this weekend.'

'Why? It'll do you good. Going anywhere nice?'

'Visiting family.'

She felt an unexpected kick of jealousy as she asked,
'You mean your children?'

'Unfortunately not.' The bitterness in his abrupt reply
was palpable, but she sensed he didn't intend to say more
as he continued almost immediately, 'Now, you are certain
you'll be OK?'

Perhaps he also had experienced tragedy in his life. Was
that why he'd understood her reluctance to talk about Jazz?
She sighed and nodded. 'No last-minute instructions?'

'Not unless the two threatened admissions give trouble.'

'They're not your problem.'

'I could wait and see them settled.'

'If it was my free weekend, I'd be gone like a shot.'

He nodded. 'I know you would and that's why I feel guilty leaving you here when your son needs you.'

'He doesn't "need" me.' She described the inverted commas round the word with her fingers. 'As I said, he'll be spoilt by his grandparents and his nanny's great.'

He frowned, then said thoughtfully, 'I could perhaps get back earlier on Sunday.'

'Don't you trust me with your patients?'

'Of course I trust you.' He looked mortified that she might believe such a thing.

'Well, take yourself off and have a restful time. You deserve it after working with those locums until I arrived.'

He nodded, opened the door to leave, then murmured, 'Good luck, Tam. I wish…'

He hesitated for a moment and then moved purposefully towards her, his arms outstretched. Already overwhelmed by his obvious unhappy feelings and his unwarranted concern for her and her son, she took a rapid step backwards, causing him to turn abruptly and stride from the office.

Ben left Tammy feeling a fool for the way she had reacted, especially when she knew it wasn't Ben's friendly embrace she was afraid of but her own reaction to it.

She sighed and snatched up the notes of the first new arrival.

'Was that Ben leaving?' Jan asked as she joined her in the office.

Tammy nodded.

'Good. I was afraid he intended to stay around when he discovered I'm off for the next two days as well.'

'I think he was, Jan, until I asked if he didn't trust me with his patients.'

'Good for you. He needs to get a life. The sooner he finds a house he likes, the better. Living in the residency is making him a workaholic.'

'He certainly didn't seem keen to go.'

Jan pursed her lips and shook her head. 'If he had a family it would be very different—we'd probably have to tie him to the place.'

'He said he was visiting family this weekend.'

'Not the kind I'm talking about. He'd love children of his own but first he needs a wife.'

'If he hasn't found one by now, he can't have been looking very hard.'

'He thought he had until just before he came here. Then she discovered her social life and her career were more important than a move to Marton and children.'

Aware that if she didn't want people talking about her she shouldn't be encouraging Jan's gossip, however fascinating, Tammy shrugged. 'Perhaps he'll soon meet someone who feels differently.'

'Ye-es.'

She saw a glint of matchmaking in Jan's narrowing eyes and rushed to change the subject. 'Now, what about these new patients?'

She handed Tammy a thick folder of case notes. 'This is Billy Old—as you can see, he's one of our regular visitors. Isn't that right, Mrs Old?'

The anxious woman holding the patient's hand nodded. 'I've never seen him as bad as this, though.'

Seeing his breathing was still distressed, despite the administration of oxygen, Tammy asked her, 'Can you tell me what's been happening?'

'He were a miner. Got dust on his lungs. His breathing's got steadily worse this last week.'

'And he's still smoking?' Jan added.

Mrs Old nodded. 'He takes no notice of what Doctor says. I've not brought his ciggies in, though.'

'That's good.'

After listening to Billy's chest and consulting the treatment chart, Tammy told him, 'Sounds like you've got an infection on top of your usual problems, as I'm sure they told you in the accident and emergency department. We'll see how you go on with these antibiotics they've started you on. At least until the lab lets us know the specific bugs.'

Billy nodded and closed his eyes.

'All right if I stay wi' 'im, Doctor?'

'Of course. But let him sleep as much as he wants and try to persuade him to have sips of fluid when he's awake.'

Tammy crossed to the desk and wrote down her findings.

'Who's next?'

'Mr Waldron. Difficulty in breathing. No history but the oxygen helps.'

'Chest X-rays?'

Jan handed them to Tammy. 'Nothing on them. This one's a puzzle.'

Determined Ben would not find anything to criticise on Monday, Tammy was meticulous in taking a medical history from him and she examined him thoroughly. When she finished she had to agree with Jan that it wasn't going to be easy to make a diagnosis, especially as Mr Waldron's breathing became distressed every time they tried him without the oxygen.

She ordered a battery of tests, many of which wouldn't be available until after the weekend, but those that were done revealed nothing. Tammy decided there was nothing else she could do but observe and monitor and leave the verdict to Mike or Ben on Monday.

In any case she was kept busy by two more new patients over the next couple of days, which necessitated John Lowe and one of the new admissions being farmed out to beds in another ward. She never stopped and as Sunday evening approached, she found herself looking forward to Ben's return more than she would have believed.

CHAPTER THREE

BEN returned early from his weekend visit to his mother's sister, his eagerness to see Tammy tempered by a niggling curiosity.

His aunt was always interested in his work and in the course of their conversation he had mentioned his new assistant.

Over the years his aunt had become as close as his mother and consequently she had sensed from his tone of voice that he was attracted to Tammy.

However, her benevolent smile had disappeared when in response to her query he had told her Tammy's surname. 'Penrose, did you say?'

'That's right. Why?'

'Have nothing more to do with her. That hussy your cousin went off with was called Penrose.'

He had groaned inwardly before saying, 'You don't know she was a hussy and even if she was, it doesn't make everyone of the same name one. Anyway, Penrose is probably Tammy's married name.'

As Tammy didn't wear a ring, he wasn't at all sure about that, but anything to deflect his aunt's venom. She had a fanatical hatred of the person she assumed had lured his cousin James away from his family.

'You'd better ask her if she knows James.'

'That would be too much of a coincidence. There must be hundreds if not thousands of Penroses in the country. Anyway...' He was about to add that Tammy's husband was dead when he stopped himself, aware that would open a can of worms that would result in a verbal onslaught for the remainder of the weekend.

Over the years he'd tried to make his aunt accept that James would probably return in his own good time, although he'd never voiced his opinion that that would probably only be when his immature cousin began to realise he had responsibilities, but she was too entrenched in her own views to listen to anything he had to say.

Her suspicions smouldered so volubly for the remainder of the weekend that he was prevented from dismissing the idea for what it was. The delusion of an unhappy woman. For once he couldn't wait to get back to the hospital.

He was on the ward Monday morning even before the day staff arrived, but there was no sign of Tammy so he sat in on the night nurse's handover report.

When it was finished Jan turned to him with a grin. 'Joining my nursing staff, are you?'

He shook his head. 'As I was awake early I figured it was the best way of discovering what's been happening in my absence.'

'Hasn't Tammy put you in the picture?'

He shook his head. 'Haven't seen her. Doesn't sound like she's had a particularly quiet time so I hope she's catching up on her sleep.'

Tammy rushed in about five minutes later and his heart contracted at the sight of her drawn face decorated with large black circles below her eyes.

She was obviously disconcerted to find him on duty before her. 'Sorry. I—I overslept.'

He pulled out a chair for her and indicated she should sit down. His eyes searched her face. 'It sounds as if you've had a hectic couple of days. You should be still sleeping. I think you should tell me what's happening and then go home.'

'I—I can't.'

He frowned, his eyes fixed on her. 'I don't see why not.'

'The ward round, of course. I need to be here.'

'I can cope with that.'

'Don't patronise me, Ben. I'm the only one who knows what's gone on all weekend. Anyway, I've plenty of paperwork to catch up on.'

She stood up and moved towards the notes trolley, staggering slightly as she did so.

He caught her arm and demanded, 'Have you had breakfast?'

Increasingly irritated, she muttered, 'No time. I overslept. Remember?'

He took the set of notes she had extracted and replaced them in the trolley. 'I prescribe breakfast before you do anything else. And this is not patronising. It's common sense. And I need to eat as well, so you can fill me in on the details while we do so. That way we won't waste time.'

His conciliatory tone made her realise how tetchy she must sound, so she tried to explain. 'I must check the patients. I—I can't—'

'You can and you will.'

She capitulated, oddly warmed by his concern for her welfare, and followed him to the canteen.

Over breakfast, she told him, 'There are three—no, four new patients to tell you about.'

'I know. I listened in on the night nurse's report.'

'You were here that early?' She felt her cheeks colouring. 'I didn't expect to see you until the ward round. Didn't you enjoy your weekend?'

He shrugged. 'Yes and no.'

'What does that mean?'

'Like the curate's egg. Good in parts.'

Too tired to appreciate his cryptic reply, Tammy shrugged and changed the subject. 'I'm enjoying this.'

'So am I. Thank goodness you agreed to update me down here. I needed this.'

A wave of disappointment washed over her as she realised it hadn't been *her* missing breakfast that had concerned him. He'd been thinking of his own stomach!

Aware it was only her complete exhaustion that had allowed her to think any different, she pushed her plate away and said, 'Thanks for that. I'm away to my paperwork. I'll see you later.'

He didn't follow and she hurried back to the ward, berating herself for the fool she was. She was allowing this man to get under her skin. The sooner she stopped behaving like a schoolgirl with a crush and concentrated on her work, the better.

Resolving to set her alarm for an even earlier time in future, she settled to enter the test results that had arrived that morning into the relevant case notes. Then she did a mini-round of her patients to make sure she was prepared for the consultant's arrival.

Ben was with Mike Rolf when he arrived for his round. She gave the information on the first patient accurately and concisely. 'Billy has improved only slightly since he was admitted, so we're continuing with the infusion of fluids into his vein, especially as he isn't drinking much.' Suddenly conscious of Ben's approving gaze resting on her, she faltered and stumbled through her answers to the couple of questions Mike asked.

When they moved on towards the second bed, Ben lifted the notes, winked at Tammy and said smoothly, 'I can tell you about this one. Dr Penrose has had a hectic weekend.' Embarrassed, Tammy knew she couldn't snatch the notes from his hand, but she did wish he would allow her to fight her own battles.

He gave the necessary information about Mr Waldron's admission and went on to explain what had been done so far. 'He's had exhaustive tests, but they haven't shown any-thing.' He handed over the results to the consultant, then pointed at something he had just written in the notes.

Mike read them, then, handing the notes to Tammy to peruse, said, 'I'll take a look at him.'

'Hello, Mr Waldron. I'm Mr Rolf. Tell me what's been happening to you?'

The patient tugged down the oxygen mask that was still assisting him to breathe more easily. 'I was watching tele-vision on Friday afternoon,' he gasped, 'when I had a coughing fit and couldn't get my breath, and it hasn't got any better since.'

'Let me take a look at you.'

After a thorough examination, he wrote in the case notes and then said, 'When were you last in hospital?'

Mr Waldron refused to meet his eyes and mumbled, 'Never.'

'I don't think that's quite true, is it?' Mike nodded to-wards Ben, who said, 'I've come across you in a couple of hospitals now.'

Tammy released the breath she had been holding. That was one thing she couldn't have known.

'I think we'll try you without the oxygen and get some-one else to come and take a look at you.'

Sam Waldron didn't reply and didn't object when the oxygen mask was removed.

Mike Rolf patted him on the shoulder. 'Just rest quietly.' As they moved on to the next bed he said to Ben and Tammy, 'Keep an eye on him and we'll discuss what action to take later.'

Much to her relief, Ben allowed Tammy to tell the con-sultant about the remainder of the new patients and when they returned to the office Mike rested a hand on her shoul-der. 'You've done well, Tammy.'

She nodded miserably. 'Apart from Mr Waldron.'

'That was a stroke of luck for us. He's obviously a consummate actor. If Ben hadn't recognised him, I'd probably have been fooled as well. It's not something we often come across in this speciality.'

Tammy was dejected. 'I can see how he could pretend the breathlessness but not why his oxygen levels were low.'

Ben raised his eyebrows. 'That's obviously how he gets his repeated admissions to hospital—he must have trained himself to breathe shallowly or perhaps hold his breath for long periods.'

'But why?'

'Who knows, Tammy? He either likes the attention or just wants a bed for the night. Get the psychiatric lot to take a look at him, Ben, but I'll be surprised if they think there's anything much wrong with him.' Mike raised a hand in farewell and left the office.

After a moment's silence Tammy muttered, 'You might have warned me.'

He looked hurt. 'Hey, I'd no idea until I glanced at him while we were at the first bed.'

'Who should I contact, then? He can't be allowed to occupy one of our beds.'

'I'll deal with it, Tam.'

'Don't call me Tam,' she snapped. 'It's Tammy. And it's not your job. It's mine.'

Jan walked into the office as she spoke. 'Temper, temper.'

'Did you know he wasn't really ill as well?'

She shook her head. 'I have to admit I was puzzled by him. But I didn't *know*. He's a very clever man.'

Tammy was slightly mollified and said, 'I'll just take another look at him, then have a word with Mr Burton about how he'll cope at home.' She was reluctant to stay in the office a moment longer. She knew she was tired and probably imagining things, but Ben had not taken his eyes off her since they'd got back to the office, making her extremely uncomfortable.

When she got to the second bed there was no sign of Mr Waldron. She popped her head round the day-room door, but he wasn't there either. Then she noticed the charts on the end of his bed were missing.

'Did you notice the chap from that bed leaving?' she asked Mr Burton, who was seated beside the bed opposite.

He nodded. 'He said the consultant had said he could walk to the bathroom. I was surprised when he took his clothes out of the locker, but presumed he was going to dress.'

'He was alone?'

Mr Burton nodded. 'Is it all right if the wife collects me when she finishes work? That'll be about four.'

'That should be fine. I'll come back and have a chat with you when I've sorted this chap out.'

The bathroom was empty and there was no sign of Sam along the main corridor. She returned to the office and said to Ben, 'Have you contacted anyone about seeing Mr Waldron?'

'I can't get them at the moment. Probably don't work Mondays!'

'I shouldn't bother, then. I think he has left. His bed and locker are empty and even his charts have gone.'

Ben leaned thoughtfully back in his chair then clapped a hand to his forehead. 'I'll try and check but I have a feeling that's what he did at the last hospital. I'd forgotten until you mentioned it.' He turned to Jan, who was updating the nursing records. 'Is this going to cause you a problem?'

She nodded. 'We'll have to initiate a search and if he can't be found, it means questions and a detailed report on what happened. I could do without that.' She sighed. 'However, I'd better get on with it.'

She left the office and Tammy started to follow her. 'Just a minute, Tammy,' Ben called.

She turned back and waited.

His gaze was still fixed on her. 'Are you OK?'

'Yes.'

'Anything I can do to help?'

She shook her head. 'I can cope. I'll see you in the out-patient clinic. One as usual, I presume?'

'Thereabouts.' He rushed on to add, 'But you don't have to be there.'

'It's part of my duties…'

'Not necessarily when you've been on call all weekend, Mike and I can manage.'

'I'll be there.'

'What about your son?'

'He's at nursery school today.' She carried on writing.

'You must miss him.'

It was a statement rather than a question and after a moment she nodded. 'Sorry, Ben. Is this important? If I'm to be ready for the clinic at one I must get on.'

'OK. I get the message.'

'Good.' He waited, but she went on writing, so he left the office wondering why he was bothering. She was a transient member of the chest team and would move on before long.

That didn't stop him later arranging with the clinic nurse to move any outpatients he thought might give Tammy problems to his own list, leaving her with mainly follow-up appointments and as few of those as possible.

He knew Percy Good was the first on her list and when Tammy rushed into the department he wasn't surprised to hear the nurse telling her that Percy hadn't turned up.

Neither was Tammy. 'Not unexpected. At least it gives me a breathing space.'

'Do you want me to contact his GP?'

'You can try but I'd lay money on him not having been there either.'

Rob White was next and already waiting, so she called him into the consulting room.

'How've you been, Rob?'

'Wheezy.'

'More than you were before the explosion?'

He nodded.

'Does the inhaler help?'

'Most times.'

'Are you back at work?'

He shook his head. 'They've told me to take as long as I feel I need.'

'Good, and you're hearing me better, aren't you?'

He nodded. 'The ear's healed fine.'

She nodded and took his latest X-ray from the envelope that came with his notes. 'That looks OK. If you move into that cubicle and take off your shirt, I'll check your chest.'

She did so and could find nothing to account for his breathlessness but, remembering how interested Ben had been in what Rob had had to tell him about the conditions in the chemical factory, she decided to ask for his advice. 'As you're a bit more wheezy, I think I'd like Dr Davey to take a look at you. You remember him, do you?'

'Good man, that.' Rob was a man of few words. Where she was concerned anyway.

'Slip your shirt back on and the moment he's free I'll have a word with him.'

She closed the communicating door between the examination and consulting room and wrote up her findings. Then she asked her clinic nurse to let her know when Ben was free. 'In the meantime, send in my next patient, would you?'

She quickly read through the next set of notes on her

desk. 'Mr Boardman,' she greeted him. 'I'm Dr Penrose. I don't think we've met before. How are you doing?'

'About the same.'

Tammy checked his notes again and saw he was another employee of the chemical works and also had asthma.

'What chemicals are you or have you been exposed to at work?'

'So many I can't remember.'

She frowned.

'But I've had asthma since I was a lad.'

She read back through his notes and saw that all this had been noted earlier.

'I'll just check how well the drugs are working, then.' She handed him a peak-flow meter and, after standing up, he gave three good blows into the mouthpiece.

She read the results with a smile. 'No problem there. We'll see you in another six months, unless you want to see us earlier.'

He grinned. 'Six months'll be plenty soon enough. Thank you all the same, Doctor.'

'Seriously, if you do have a problem in the meantime, let us know.'

'I will, Doc, I will. Especially if it's you I'll see. You're prettier than Dr Rolf!'

Tammy was noting down her findings when Ben appeared in the doorway. 'Sandra says you want to see me.'

'It's about Rob White. He's more breathless than when he left us. His X-ray looks OK but I thought perhaps you ought to see him.'

He nodded. 'Thanks. In here?' He indicated the examination-room door.

'Yep. Do you want me to come?'

'I'll call if I need you.'

He was back before long. 'We'll see him again in a couple of weeks but I think it's just that he's doing more now he's home. Still, I'm glad you asked me to check him over. He's a mine of information.'

'About the explosion?'

'About the factory conditions in general. Interesting.'

'The last chap I saw worked there as well. Do most of Mike's patients?'

'More than is healthy.' Realising what he'd just said, he chuckled. 'If you know what I mean. Seriously, Mike and I are looking into the conditions there with one of the inspectors.' With that he went back to his own consulting room, leaving Tammy to see a couple of men who'd had bad chest infections but were now fine and could be signed off the hospital books.

'No one else?' she asked Sandra.

'You've got an easy afternoon. Dr Davey said he'd see the remainder that were on your list.'

Was this another instance of him not trusting her or was it one more example of his philanthropy?

When he'd finished the clinic Ben went back to the ward, hoping Tammy had managed to get away and yet half hoping she would still be there.

She was attending to paperwork in the office. 'I thought you'd have left long before this. You must be exhausted.'

'Not much more to do. I'm just completing my report on Mr Waldron.'

'We could have wasted a lot of time there if I hadn't recognised him.'

'Mmm!'

Ben hesitated, then said, 'Talking about recognising people, have you ever come across a James Walton?

She shook her head. 'Is he another phoney hypochondriac?'

'No. He's my cousin.'

'Your cousin? Why on earth should I know *him*?'

'My aunt believes he was lured away from home by a wicked woman by the name of Penrose.'

She snapped her head up and looked at him. 'Well, it wasn't me. I've never even heard of him.'

'I didn't expect you would have. You're not wicked enough.'

'Is that a compliment?'

He grinned. 'Perhaps a complaint. What do you think?'

Unnerved by the seductive gleam in his eyes, she snapped, 'That I'm too tired to solve your riddles and as I'm just about finished here, I'm going home to Jake.'

She lifted her belongings and was gone before he could reply.

Tammy made her way to her car, conscious that she had done nothing to endear herself to Ben, but she was tired. So when he looked at her like that her imagination ran away with her and she couldn't trust herself. He was too attractive by half.

As she turned into the drive of the semi-detached house that was home, she thrust all thought of Clarke Ward and Ben Davey from her mind.

Jake's welcome was exuberant as usual. When she could at last disentangle herself, she said, 'Hi, Lauren. All well?'

'Fine. I've put a casserole in the oven so you can eat with Jake.'

'You're a star, Lauren. Thank you. Are you eating with us?'

Lauren shook her head. 'Marcus is taking me out for a meal this evening.'

'He knows you, Mummy.' Determined to grab her attention, Jake had thrust himself headlong into her.

'Steady on, Jake. You nearly knocked me over.'

'Marcus knows you, Mummy. I'm trying to tell you.'

Tammy looked towards Lauren, and raised a querying eyebrow.

'He works at the chemical factory. He's a manager there. One of his men was in your ward.'

Suddenly enlightened, Tammy nodded. 'If I've got the right person, he collected one of our patients when he was discharged.'

'That's right, he did.' Lauren paused, before saying hesitantly, 'He—he says your doctors are out to make trouble for him.'

'I don't think so, Lauren. They're just concerned about the men working there. I think they are working with the management rather than against them.'

'Come on, Mummy-y.' Jake was pulling her by one arm towards the playroom.

Tammy gave Lauren a rueful look and followed him.

The nanny didn't follow and Tammy let the subject drop. This was Jake's time and she intended to give her full attention to him until it was time to return to the hospital the next morning.

'Look at my painting—I drew you and Marcus and Lauren.'

He handed her a sheet of paper with three garish, unrecognisable blobs. 'Tell me about them,' she suggested, lifting him onto her knee. He pointed at the green oblong. 'That's you, Mummy, and this is Lauren—see, she's higher than you.'

'She's quite a bit *taller* than me, isn't she?' she corrected his mistake gently. 'Did you do these with Lauren?'

'No. At nursery.'

'It's a lovely painting. I'll put it up on the pinboard, shall I?'

Jake nodded. 'I'm hungry, Mummy.'

'Let's go and find this casserole.'

By the time they'd finished their meal, it was Jake's bath-and bedtime. By the time that was finished and she had read three bedtime stories, Tammy was ready for bed herself.

She cleared the dishes, downloaded and answered a couple of important emails and, after luxuriating in a hot shower, was soon asleep herself.

Morning came much sooner than she would have believed possible. The alarm woke her at six and she climbed from her bed, wishing she didn't have to.

When she was ready to leave she peeped in at Jake and smiled tenderly as she saw he was sleeping soundly despite lying across the bed horizontally. Lauren came out of the room next door and whispered, 'You off now?'

'Yes. Did you have a good time last night?'

'Great, thanks.'

'I'll ring you later. I should be home reasonably early tonight.'

Lauren nodded and was already on her way back into her own room as Tammy closed the door.

She felt peevish as she climbed into her small Peugeot car. Why should everyone else be allowed to sleep on when it was her who had been awake most of the weekend?

Her black thoughts disappeared as she arrived at the hospital and greeted her colleagues, many as bleary-eyed as herself. She even felt buoyant when the night nurse, Di Lennard, greeted her with the news that for once they'd had a quiet night and there was nothing urgent to be done.

She did a quick round of the patients, many of whom were dozing, and, having checked all their charts, she then went down to the canteen for coffee.

Ben was at a table in the corner and smiled a greeting which, despite all her efforts to the contrary, left her aware of a pleasurable tightening of her nerve endings. He moved dirty dishes aside so that she could join him.

'Quiet night?' she asked, trying to ignore the flood of warmth his smile had provoked.

He nodded. 'Seven full hours' sleep, would you believe? I keep wondering what I'm going to find when I get up to the ward.'

'Nothing untoward. I've checked.'

'What unearthly time did you get here?'

'About an hour ago.'

'Guilty conscience?'

'Oh! I'm…' Remembering her abrupt departure the previous evening, she was about to apologise when she saw his teasing smile was accompanying what she could see now was light-hearted banter. 'No. Just conditioned by lots of early mornings with Jake. Lovable as they are, children do have their downside.'

The moment she'd uttered the words and saw the sadness in his face, she remembered what Jan had said about him wanting a family and regretted having spoken.

'I'm a lark in the mornings so I don't think it would be a hardship to me. But…' he lifted a shoulder hopelessly '…I'll never know now.'

Guilty at the distress she had caused him by her throwaway remark, Tammy swallowed hard. 'Whyever not?'

'My partner had other priorities and so she upped and left.'

Although he was making light of it, it was startlingly clear to Tammy at that moment just how badly he had been hurt.

'Had you been together long?' she asked, gently resting her hand on his arm.

'Nearly five years. And never the merest hint she didn't want a family.'

'Perhaps she'd only just realised…'

He shook his head. 'No. I was a fool where Deanna was concerned.'

Sensing his despair, she murmured gently, 'We all make mistakes. Give it time.'

He stared at her silently for long seconds, then said brusquely, 'That's something our work doesn't allow us enough of. Drink up. Clarke Ward calls.'

Tammy guessed he was now embarrassed by his revelation and wanted to steer the conversation away from his problems, so she took a sip of her coffee and said, 'Mmm. I needed that caffeine.'

He gave her a grateful smile and pushed a plate of buttered toast towards her. 'Help yourself.'

'I can't eat yours.'

'My eyes were bigger than my stomach so your help would be appreciated.'

She took a piece and nibbled at it slowly. 'That's good, thanks.'

An uneasy silence settled between them before Tammy started to say, 'Why is it—?' She broke off because he'd spoken at the same moment. 'You first.'

'Nothing important. Just idle curiosity.'

'Fire away.'

'What time *did* Jake get you up?'

'I kept him up later than usual last night so he was still sleeping when I left.'

'I expect he'd missed you. What were you about to say just now?'

'Why is it that some medics always get quiet nights on call and others usually have busy ones?'

'Somebody or other's law, I suppose. You're one of the unlucky ones?'

She nodded. 'Seems like it.'

'Perhaps we should do a swap.'

She laughed. 'I've tried it. It doesn't work.' She handed her mug to the girl clearing the tables. 'Time I was moving.'

Ben accompanied her back to the ward and, relieved that

after a sticky patch their former camaraderie was returning, she looked forward to the day ahead.

Jan met them in the corridor and asked Tammy if she could check Billy Old's infusion site. 'I think he's tugged it out of the vein.'

Tammy wrinkled her nose. 'Not again. I thought the splint had cured that problem once and for all.'

Ben laughed. 'Call me if there's a problem, Tammy.'

The moment they were alone in the office Jan said to Ben, 'I see she's forgiven you.'

'Forgiven me?' He frowned.

'I thought you said she didn't like you prying into her private life.'

'Goodness, Jan. That was on her first day.'

'So you know all about her now?'

Aware that Jan was looking for any titbits of gossip she could pass on, he said, 'No. We've called a truce.'

'Why? Does she have something to hide?'

He gave an exasperated shrug of his shoulders. 'I've no idea, Jan, but if she has it's nothing to do with us.'

'Defending her now? My, you are smitten.'

Ben glared and snatched open the office door. As he made his way out, Jan laughed. 'And now you've just confirmed it.'

He swung round. 'What did I do to deserve working with a Gestapo agent?' He strode into the ward to see if Tammy needed any help.

'I'd like you to take a look at this, Ben.' She indicated Billy Old's arm and held out his fluid balance chart. 'I think precious little of the fluid has gone into his vein. Can we dispense with the drip now he's taking more fluids orally?'

'I should think so, as long as there's someone around to make sure he continues to drink enough. Here. Let me help you.'

He held the arm whilst she placed a pressure dressing

over the needle site. As she fixed it in place she was conscious of her hand brushing Ben's. The contact made heat flood into her cheeks and she averted her head in the hope it wouldn't be noticed.

No such luck. Jan joined them at that moment and drew attention to Tammy's cheeks by asking, 'What's the blush in aid of?'

They both ignored the question and Ben told her, 'Billy's fluid intake must be kept up or this'll have to go back up again. You hear that, Mr Old? You need to drink at least two glasses of water an hour.'

The patient looked at them blankly.

Ben sighed. 'He's not taking it in, is he? Keep an eye on him, will you, Jan?'

She nodded. 'I came to ask you about transferring back some of your sleepers.'

'I think we'll keep that empty bed available for the moment. Surprisingly Mr Wilbur has done really well and ICU want to free up one of theirs.'

The office was empty when he eventually returned and he sat down to think about what Jan had said earlier. The trouble was, Tammy *had* got under his skin. She held a definite attraction for him, yet he couldn't get what his aunt had told him out of his mind. And it was so ridiculous.

He sighed, aware that for his aunt's sake he needed to know for certain so that he could convince her once and for all there was no connection.

He owed her that for all they had done for him over the years when his own father and mother had more often than not been out of the country. His aunt and uncle had never made any distinction between him and their own son, so James had been like a brother to him. It had been hard for all of them when James had quarrelled violently with his father over his career and had left home.

Like his uncle before his death, Ben wasn't convinced a

girl was to blame. But nothing he could say would persuade his aunt otherwise, and if he didn't go back with conclusive proof she would leave no stone unturned to try and find out the truth about Tammy for herself.

The object of his thoughts came into the office at that moment. 'Good timing,' he greeted her.

'For what?'

'To go through the duty rotas and arrange our evening out.'

'Our evening…'

'You did promise.'

She sighed. 'I know. But I'm on call again tomorrow and it looks as if you are at the weekend.'

'That leaves tonight or Thursday.'

'No way, sorry. I— Those evenings are for Jake.'

'What about later? When he's in bed?'

She hesitated before saying reluctantly, 'I'll need to check with Lauren. She knows my rota and may have made arrangements to go out. When I've done this I'll ring Lauren and check.'

Before she had a chance to do so, the nurse in charge of the admissions ward rang to ask for help. 'I've a chap just arrived here in status asthmaticus and by rights he should go to ITU but they haven't a bed. Could you come and take a look at him?'

She relayed the message to Ben. 'Sounds like we're going to fill that empty bed.'

He grimaced. 'If he's that bad, he ought to go to the nearest ITU with available beds. I'll go and take a look at him. I'll ring if I need you.'

His call wasn't long coming. 'Could you tell Jan we'll admit this chap? His condition is already stabilising. I'll come up with him.'

Tammy was still busy with her paperwork when they arrived and Ben came into the office. 'Klaus is an artist—

highly strung and over-anxious, as many artists seem to be. Probably that and starving in a freezing garret is the cause of this exacerbation. He doesn't remember being as bad as this before.'

'So what's been done and what needs to be?'

He handed her the treatment sheet. 'As you saw, he's on continuous oxygen and has had nebulised salbutamol and started on a course of steroids. I've suggested continuing treatment providing he keeps on improving. Apart from monitoring his peak-flow level, there's nothing urgent to be done at the moment, except keep an eye on him and tell him to go out and get a proper job.'

Surprised by such an outburst from the normally mild-mannered Ben, she rushed to the defence of artists. 'You never know, he might be the next Picasso.' Without waiting for a response, she picked up a peak-flow meter and made her way into the ward. 'I'll see if he can manage this yet.'

It wasn't until much later that she had a moment to ring home. Lauren was more than happy to stay in with Marcus, so when she saw Ben again, Tammy offered to meet him.

'Half-eight or ninish? We're both working tomorrow so that should allow us to get home at a reasonable hour.'

'That's fine by me. I'll pick you up around half-eight, then.'

She shook her head. 'You tell me where and when and I'll be there. I like to have my own car in case Jake needs me.'

CHAPTER FOUR

SEATED outside The Cricketers, Ben checked his watch and not for the first time wondered if Tammy was going to turn up. She had an elusive quality that intrigued him and he hoped that if he got to know more about her he would understand the reason for it.

When he'd said he'd pick her up she'd made the excuse that she must have her own transport in case Jake needed her. But that was a feeble excuse—what would she do if there was an emergency with Jake when she was on duty? She couldn't just cut and run. So did she feel the need for an escape route? He didn't think he'd given her any cause for that.

With relief he saw her car turn into the road and went to greet her in the car park.

'Everything OK at home?'

She nodded. 'Sorry about the time. I don't like to rush Jake.'

'No problem. I booked a table.'

While Ben was queuing to order their food, Tammy studied him intently and decided it was worth ignoring her reservations to have such an imposing companion for the evening.

When he'd mentioned arranging this meal immediately after their discussion over breakfast, she'd panicked, wondering if he believed her sympathy had been an offer of herself as a successor to Deanna. Because that was not what she had intended. Involvement with any man was the last thing she was looking for, and it would be the worst thing she could do to someone who already had a jaundiced view of women, especially those with careers.

'That took a long time, but I'm assured the food won't be too long.' Ben had rejoined her at the table.

She smiled. 'No hurry. It's lovely just to sit quietly for a few moments.'

'It must be hard not to be able to put your feet up when you get home.'

'Jake's worth it.'

'Was his father a medic?'

'Oh, no. He—he'd just finished university. He was still looking for work when he was killed.' After the comments Ben had made about artists when Klaus had been admitted, she preferred to tell him Jazz had been unemployed, which was the truth.

'What kind of work?'

'He wasn't sure what he was going to do. Certainly nothing in the medical world.'

He frowned. 'How long had you been together?'

She shrugged. 'Not long.'

'So you weren't married...?' He allowed the question to trail off as he lightly touched her empty ring finger.

She took a deep breath. 'I can see you've already worked it out. No. We weren't.'

No proof for his aunt there, then. Her maiden name *was* Penrose.

She could sense her answer wasn't what he had expected, so she told him, 'I had my studies to concentrate on. It just never seemed a priority.'

He rested a sympathetic hand over hers, sending a tremulous warmth to the pit of her stomach and making her feel guilty at what she was omitting to tell him, but blackening Jazz's name wouldn't reflect particularly well on her either. Best to change the subject.

'Having Jake has helped a lot.'

'I can imagine. How did you and Jake's father meet?'

'At a student rag. We were both in a group trying to raise money by getting to Paris without it costing us a penny.'

'Quite an undertaking these days. Did you succeed?'

'Not exactly for free but we got there and raised a goodly sum for St Mungo's.'

'I imagine working together for a good cause would make a firm base for any relationship.'

'It did seem to.' No point in telling him that she'd discovered later that Jazz had only joined in the rag stunt for his own ends—he'd wanted to visit the Left Bank—and, worse still, had never handed over the money he'd raised. Much to her embarrassment.

'You must have proud memories.'

Her reply was a noncommittal 'Hmm'.

Ben reached across and grasped both her hands. 'Why do I feel there is something you're not telling me—holding back?'

She looked down at their joined hands and sighed at his perception. 'It was a difficult time and I'd rather not talk about it.' She raised her head and the compassion she saw in his eyes brought tears to the back of her eyes.

'Did you grow up in Marton?' He squeezed her hands gently as he spoke.

Tammy sent him a grateful smile for a question that allowed her to regain her composure and dismiss unhappy memories. 'Born and bred here.'

'Where did you go to school?'

'The local primary and then on to the comprehensive on the outskirts of town. It was the only one at that time.'

He nodded. 'I gather Marton has grown a lot in recent years.'

'Not very recent—it spread when I was still at school.'

'Your parents have always lived here?' He released her hands as he reached for his drink.

'Yes, and my grandparents. I'm a local girl through and through.'

'It must be comforting to have your extended family around you. So many new mothers miss out on that these days.'

She nodded. 'I must say it has been a help. Even though they're all out at work.'

'Not at the chemical factory, I hope.'

She laughed. 'No. Mum's a practice manager and—'

'Ah—that's where you inherited the medical interest from. And your father?'

'He has a small engineering firm that makes components for the aircraft industry.' She paused as the food was put before them. 'Penrose Electronics on the industrial estate.'

'I was tempted by engineering. If I hadn't done medicine, that's what I'd be.'

'I suppose the two careers are vaguely analogous—as doctors we look after human machinery.'

'How true. And now…' he indicated the food that remained untouched since being brought to their table a few moments before '…I suggest we eat some of this before it goes cold.'

'I've been talking too much.'

'It's my fault for asking too many questions.'

He watched her thoughtfully while she ate. Her open responses about the family she had grown up in had surprised him. Her forthcoming answers were such a contrast to her evasiveness about the man who'd fathered her child.

Over coffee she prompted, 'What about you? Where was your home?'

'You could really say I had no fixed abode.'

She frowned. 'No fixed abode?'

'My father worked for an overseas bank and he and my

mother spent my young life moving round the capital cities of the world. Now they've settled in Hong Kong.'

'How fantastic—what an education, seeing how people in other countries live.'

'Er, I didn't. I said my parents—not me. I was dumped in a boarding school at the youngest age they would accept me and I saw them on their brief forays home.'

His bitterness at his upbringing was obvious.

'So what about the school holidays?'

'Mum's sister and her husband gave me a home—they were very good to me. I was treated like a second son.'

'They're obviously kind people. Do you see them much these days?'

'My aunt lives not all that far from Marton. Her husband died a few months ago so I try to visit whenever I can.'

'And their own son? Where's he?'

'He was the cousin I mentioned to you. James. He refused to study law so that he could join the family firm. After a blazing row my uncle bawled him out and he left home and hasn't been heard of since.'

'That's awful, Ben.' Tammy was visualising how traumatic it would be if Jake disappeared from her life.

'I try to soften the loss by visiting my aunt as often as possible—in fact, that's where I went last weekend. But it's not easy.'

'Not easy?' Tammy frowned. 'In what way?'

'His mother believed he would never come back while his father was alive, but she sees no reason for him not to now. She'll stop at nothing to find him.'

'I'm beginning to see why you were glad to get back to work on Monday.'

'Don't get me wrong—she's kindness itself to me, but she's just got too much time to sit and think.'

Tammy nodded, then said slowly. 'I don't think I'd ever give up either. Has she any leads?'

'Only this girl she seems to have a bee in her bonnet about. But I've never believed anyone would persuade James to do anything he didn't want to. Neither did his father.'

'But his mother doesn't agree with you.'

'Mothers are...' He hesitated then grinned wryly. 'Methinks I need to be careful here.'

'You think we're naïve?'

He shook his head. 'Not naïve, no, more that they are a little too close to their children, especially sons. And before you shoot me down, let me add that I think fathers are probably the same with their daughters. Think they can do no wrong.'

'That's what you believe?'

'You watch. If a child gets into serious trouble the mother is always convinced that he must have been led astray by friends.'

Tammy raised a hand to hide a smile as she recalled saying something similar when Lauren had told her Jake had refused to allow a new boy to join his group of friends in the nursery class.

'You could be right.'

'So, we know a lot more about one another now.' Ben reached across and took hold of one of her hands. 'And that can only be a good thing because I hope we'll be seeing a lot more of one another in the future. And not just at work.' His voice had dropped to a seductive murmur which churned her insides with a mixture of excitement and panic—excitement because he was a man she was increasingly attracted to and panic because she wasn't ready for any kind of a relationship.

To hide her hesitancy, she avoided his questioning gaze and looked down at the mesmerising caress of his thumb on her palm.

'Are you happy about that?'

Tammy wasn't sure about that. Since the day they'd met she'd been conscious of a heightened awareness between them which she'd tried to ignore. She'd been there with Jazz and had to count the cost.

'Tammy?' She raised her head slowly to meet his eyes watching her with a puzzled expression. 'If it's the memory of Jake's father that's preventing you from answering,' he told her softly, 'I'm sure he wouldn't object to us being friends.'

'No. He wouldn't. I suppose it's just— I've only been at the hospital for a couple of weeks and, well, it's early days yet and I'm not sure...' She swallowed hard. If that was all he was suggesting, no problem. 'Yes. I'd like that.'

'I'm glad about that.' Ben checked his watch. 'Where does the time go? I'd better settle the bill and get you home to your son and your beauty sleep. And, Tammy...'

'Yes?'

'I'd like to meet Jake.'

She nodded. 'I'm sure we can arrange that some time.'

He released her hand and pushed back his chair. 'You're sure you don't want any more coffee?'

She shook her head. 'No, thanks.'

As they walked to the car park at the rear of the building he slung an arm loosely around her shoulders. When she stopped at her car, he leaned towards her and his lips touched first her forehead, then her lips. The gentle pressure of his firm lips, together with the tantalising taste of him, released such a storm of repressed longing within her that, trembling, she pulled back from him.

He ran the back of his hand gently down her cheek. 'You must have loved him very much.' His voice was soft. 'Drive carefully and sleep well. I'll see you in the morning.'

He opened her car door so that she could climb inside and, having started the engine, she had to force herself to concentrate on her driving.

He'd got it so wrong. It wasn't because she'd loved Jazz that she was so wary of a new liaison. It was because *he* hadn't loved her or the child she'd been carrying that she now expected every man she met to act in a similar way.

She arrived home to find the house quiet, much to her relief. She wanted to think things through and try to regain control of her emotions.

After checking on Jake, she crept into bed, her mind working overtime. Ben was obviously attracted to her but she wasn't ready to make another mistake and that was what she felt it would be if she allowed him any closer at this time. By the morning she was none the wiser, apart from knowing she had missed a whole night's sleep and was exhausted!

Jake woke as she moved about her room so, yawning, she took him downstairs and started on breakfast for them both.

'Mummy, do you *have* to go to work today?' he asked wistfully.

'I'm afraid so, love. I can't let my patients down.'

He stuck out his bottom lip. 'You won't work tonight as well, will you? Please, Mum.'

'I'm sorry, love.' She cuddled him close. 'I have to. But I promise I'll try and get home early tomorrow.'

She saw tears collecting in his eyes. 'Lauren will be here to look after you.'

He sniffed. 'But I'd much rather have you.'

She wiped his nose automatically. 'And I'd rather it was me here with you, but that's just not possible for the time being.'

'Why?' Making snuffling noises that made her blink back tears herself, he buried his face in the fabric of her skirt. She was already getting late for work, but she couldn't leave him in such an upset state. She lifted him into her arms and hugged him.

Much to her relief, Lauren joined them and with no sign at all of his earlier tears, Jake turned his attention to asking her if they could go to the playing field after nursery school.

Her heart heavy, Tammy knew he was always fine the moment she was out of the door, but she had to admit she was growing increasingly reluctant to leave him.

As she climbed into her car she resolved, not for the first time, to try and work as few hours as was possible once she was established as a GP. Children grew up far too quickly and she'd already missed enough of Jake's milestones.

Once again Ben had beaten her in the early rising stakes. She knew living in the residency made it easier for him to get there, but when it was her job to arrive first and discover what was happening, his repeated early starts wrongfooted her.

'Couldn't you sleep either?' she snapped, somewhat ungraciously blaming him for her loss of sleep.

'I had the best night's sleep I've had for a long time.' He grinned. 'I take it you didn't?'

'Not really.'

'Your son?'

'No. He sleeps well. But he didn't want me to leave this morning. He was fine once Lauren appeared.'

He nodded his understanding but, although he said no more, she sensed he disapproved. Tough. She didn't leave him out of choice.

'I listened in to the hand-over report again and nothing seems to have changed much from last night.'

'Thanks but I'll do a quick round of the patients anyway. I prefer to check for myself.'

'I'll come with you. If that's OK?'

'Fine,' she told him shortly wondering if anything would

dent his unfailing enthusiasm for his work. Then, feeling guilty, she added, 'I guess two heads are better than one.'

As it happened, within seconds of entering the ward she was very glad indeed that Ben was there.

Julie, one of the newer care assistants on the ward, called them over to see Mr Wood, admitted the day before because his chronic chest problem had become complicated by infection.

'He's coughing up blood,' she greeted them in a panic.

'Have you saved it?'

She shook her head.

'Pity we didn't see how much blood there was,' he murmured under his breath as they made their way to the patient's bedside. 'He started his intravenous antibiotics twenty-four hours ago, didn't he?'

Tammy nodded. 'And should have had a repeat X-ray this morning.'

'He has.'

It was all Tammy could do not to mutter 'Clever clogs' even though she knew he was trying to make things easier for her. Instead she watched as he rechecked Mr Wood's observations and carefully listened to his chest before saying to the obviously anxious man, 'That sounds so much better I can't believe it was anything too serious. We'll take a look at your latest X-ray and then get back to you.'

They both returned to the office and as Tammy retrieved the packet of films and slotted the latest one into the viewing machine she said, 'That blood didn't come from his chest, did it?'

Ben shook his head. 'I don't think so. Have we got the blood-test results yet?'

Tammy riffled through the papers in her in tray. 'Doesn't look like it.'

'Chase them up. Urgently. Just in case. But what I think has happened is that his persistent coughing has caused damage to the surface of his airways. It probably wasn't that much but scary to a novice like Julie and I guess she panicked the patient. We need to have a word with Jan about training her newest recruit.'

When she had tracked down the results, she handed her jottings to Ben.

He looked up at her with a teasing grin. 'Very neat writing for a doctor's scribbling.'

She felt her cheeks colour as she retorted, 'I'd noticed yours is practically illegible!'

'You children bickering again?' Jan admonished with a grin. 'What are you doing about Mr Wood?'

'Suggesting you train your new staff not to panic at the sight of a drop of blood,' he retorted.

Completely unfazed, Jan nodded. 'You think that's all it was? I rather thought that might be the case when she told me just now.'

'I'm just on my way to have a chat with him. Put his mind at rest.' Tammy hurried out of the office, annoyed at giving Jan something to gossip about.

Mr Wood looked at her anxiously as she reached him so she gave him a reassuring smile and settled on the chair at his bedside.

'Your latest X-ray shows you're responding well to the drugs. We think all the coughing you've been doing has probably ruptured a small blood vessel. If it happens again, tell the nurse to keep it for me to see but, judging by the pictures and how well your chest sounds, I'm sure there's nothing to worry about.'

He didn't look convinced and his fingers tugged nervously at the oxygen mask he was wearing.

'Is something else worrying you?'

He nodded and pulled the mask aside. 'My brother-in-law had the same.'

'Chest infection?'

'That's what they said at first—then he coughed up blood like that. When they took a look it was cancer.'

'We've seen enough pictures of your lungs to know that's not so in your case. I'm sure Mr Rolf warned you that the chronic airways disease would have weakened your chest, letting you pick up chest infections easily.'

He nodded. 'He did.'

'That's what happened here and it's well on the way to being knocked on the head. We'll continue the intravenous antibiotics for a little while longer then you'll probably be able to go home.'

'You're not just saying that?'

Tammy shook her head. 'I'm telling you the truth.' She watched the relief spread to his eyes and patted his hand before getting to her feet. 'You'll soon begin to feel much better.'

'I do already, Doctor. You're a miracle-worker, no doubt about it. Thank you.'

When she returned to the office Jan raised a questioning eyebrow.

'He feels better already.'

'We aim to please.' She grinned. 'No time to rest on our laurels, though. There's another admission on his way up from A and E. Ben's down there with him.'

Mr Burt arrived a moment later, accompanied by Ben.

Jan indicated that the first bed in the ward was prepared to receive him.

While he was being transferred, Ben told Tammy, 'His name's Stan—seems he has quite a few problems.'

'Chest X-ray and blood-gas levels?'

'All done.' He handed Tammy the results.

'Already one of our patients?'

Ben shook his head. 'Just moved here to be near his daughter. His GP has written for an appointment. Poor chap has quite a few problems.' He handed her the notes he had made which also told her the drugs given so far. 'He's responding slowly but needs to continue the high level of oxygen for the time being. We'll see how he goes from here.'

Tammy kept a close eye on him whilst continuing her other work. When he seemed a little more comfortable she decided to try him with a peak-flow meter.

'I expect you've tried one of these before.'

He took it from her, zeroed it and blew into it before handing it back to her.

'Not bad,' she told him, although the reading was much lower than it should have been. 'When you're ready, try again.'

He blew into the machine twice more but the readings remained much the same. 'OK. That's fine,' she reassured him. 'I think we'll continue with the oxygen for the time being, though.'

She asked him a few more questions and discovered that he'd had asthma since his childhood and had then worked with asbestos for nearly forty years.

'You use inhalers at home.'

He nodded and pointed to his current ones which were on his bedside locker.

'Anything else?'

Stan shook his head.

'And they've controlled it until now?'

He shrugged his shoulders.

Tammy frowned. 'Do you have a nebuliser at home?'

He was clearly puzzled.

Tammy reached across to lift down the nebuliser. 'Like this. You used one when you first arrived at the hospital. It delivers the drugs in a fine liquid spray and is much more efficient than your inhaler.'

'I didn't know what it was called.'

Tammy could sense her questioning was becoming

stressful to him so she said, 'Not to worry. You'll be using one regularly for the next couple of days. The nurses will make sure you're doing it right.'

She returned to the office to write up her notes about him.

Ben joined her there and read over her shoulder. 'Poor chap. I don't think there's much we can do for him but treat the symptoms.'

She nodded and, handing him the prescription sheet she had just completed, asked 'Is that regime OK?'

He scanned it and said, 'Fine. We'll see how he goes before deciding the way forward.'

'I'm on call so perhaps I'll be able to decide later tonight.'

'I'm sorry about that.'

She swung round and glared at him. 'Sorry! You still don't trust me.'

He caught her lightly in his arms. 'Hey, hey, of course I do. I think you're supremely capable. I'm just sorry you have to have another night away from your son.'

Tammy's fury subsided as quickly as it had flared. 'I've worked with so many chauvinistic doctors that I tend to defend myself even when no criticism is meant.'

Jan banged open the office door at that moment and then stopped in her tracks. 'Well, well, sorry to disturb your tryst but I need to check Mr Wilbur's notes for the tablets he needs to take home.'

Tammy, who had broken away from Ben at the first click of the handle, felt a fiery heat wash over her cheeks. Jan couldn't have seen anything, could she? Or was it that they both looked guilty?

'What are you suggesting, Sister?' Ben laughed. 'We were just having another friendly difference of opinion.'

'Hmm. You seem to have a lot of those.'

'Tammy accused me of being a male chauvinist.'

At Jan's peal of laughter, Tammy felt the heat that had been subsiding creep back again. 'That isn't what I said at all,' she protested.

'I should hope not. Ben's so easygoing that he even tolerates the nursing staff telling him what to do.'

'I must get on.' Tammy snatched up a set of notes and hurried into the ward, with Ben's laughter following.

The trouble was that he was too easygoing, and likable—too likable. As Jan had intimated, he was a pleasure to work with and he would, no doubt, be a pleasure to live with—but that was the last thing she should be thinking about.

Ben smiled ruefully at Jan. 'Methinks that girl's been through more than she's letting on. She scuttles away from kindness like a startled deer.'

'You really are smitten, aren't you?'

'I like her and I'm impressed by her work. I'm not sure about smitten. I'm intrigued more than anything.'

'She's a very private person, isn't she? She doesn't chat with any of us about what she does in her spare time and who she's been out with, like the rest of us do.'

'Yes and no. I sense she's more frightened than secretive and I wish I knew what of.' He had no intention of revealing the fact that Tammy had a child. Even though he thought she was making a mistake not telling everyone about Jake. It would make the people she worked with a lot more sympathetic towards her. Now they all considered her aloof.

At least he felt he was beginning to break down some of the barriers. He'd learnt a little more about her the previous evening, even if it was mostly about her childhood and parents. Although she still wasn't willing to talk as openly about Jake's father.

Which had set his own mind at rest once and for all. She couldn't possibly be talking about his cousin. When he'd last seen him, James had been immature and had cared about no one but himself. Unless meeting Tammy had wrought a miracle, his aunt was definitely wrong in imagining Tammy could be the girl who had lured James from his home. Because if James had changed so much he'd have been home again long before this.

Ben saw Tammy only briefly during the remainder of the day, so was again early on duty the next morning to see what kind of a night she had had. True to form, it had been hectic.

Two new patients had been admitted and one had died after a couple of hours. Mr Burt was worse—upset by the commotion in the bed next to him—and now he seemed to be developing a chest infection.

'Did you get to bed at all?'

She nodded. 'A couple of hours.'

'Tell me what's happening and then get your head down for the morning.'

'I can't. Mike might do a round and want to know about these new patients.'

'No need. I'll be there.'

'I'd rather stay, Ben. I've survived much longer hours.'

'Maybe, but you're going off early this afternoon.'

'If you insist, I certainly won't argue. But it'll be just my luck for us to be so busy by that time that it won't be possible.'

'Now, there's a challenge.'

'What are we doing tomorrow, Mummy?' Jake asked as she was putting him to bed on Friday evening.

'What would you like to do?'

'Go to the park.'

'You do that most days with Lauren.'

'I want to show you the new slide with steps and ropes. I can slide down on the rope now, Mummy. I couldn't at first, and Lauren had to hold me, but I can do it on my own now.'

He was bursting with pride at his achievement so Tammy hugged him tight and said, 'Of course you can show me. I can't wait to see how clever you are.'

'Will Lauren come, too?'

Tammy shook her head. 'She's away visiting a friend until Sunday evening.'

'But *can* we go in the morning?'

'As soon as you're awake and have had breakfast.'

Tammy realised next morning that it had been a big mistake to say that. Jake was awake and dressed by six and had poured his own cereal out by the time she staggered downstairs.

At least there was a bonus to being up and about early. They had the playground to themselves. It was a fine and not too cold morning, and Tammy enjoyed the brisk walk to the park as much as a very excited Jake. He raced up the steps and down the rope over and over again, occasionally alternating it with a trip down the slide.

When he eventually began to lose interest, she asked, 'Shall we go home for a drink and a biscuit now?'

'Can I see where you go every day?' he demanded. 'Lauren won't show me.'

Tammy could see no harm in letting him see the building. 'We can't go in, though. Just walk along the street beside it.'

As they approached the new building that was the hospital, Jake demanded, 'What do you do in there?'

'I look after people who are ill.'

'Like I was when I had the spots?' He'd had chickenpox six months before but to Tammy's relief it had been a very mild dose.

'Something like that, but sometimes they feel so ill that

they need to stay in bed. Then we can look after them. You had Lauren to look after you, didn't you?'

He nodded and stopped to watch an ambulance roar through the gates, its blue lights flashing. 'Why is it doing that and not going nee-naw?' He tried to imitate the wailing siren of emergency vehicles.

'They don't want to disturb the patient with the siren, even though they need to get to the hospital quickly.'

'So that they can be looked after by you?'

'Not just me. Hundreds of people work there. But not me today. I'm staying with you, and I think it's time we went back home for that drink.'

He nodded his agreement and they turned to go back the way they had come, but they didn't get far. A young girl was hunched up against the wall, gasping for breath.

Tammy looked around but there was no one else about. 'Sit down by the wall for a minute,' she ordered Jake, 'and don't move till I tell you.'

She crouched down in front of the girl.

'Asthma?'

The girl nodded.

'Inhaler?'

This time the girl gestured towards her bag beside her on the pavement.

Tammy looked inside but the only salbutamol inhaler was empty. However, the girl did have a mobile phone. Tammy seized on it with relief. 'Can I ring for help?'

She nodded. Tammy rang the hospital number, then tapped in the special code that allowed her to get straight through to Ben's bleeper number.

He answered almost immediately.

'Ben. It's Tam. I'm at the main hospital gate with my son and there's a girl here collapsed with a bad asthma attack. Can you organise help?'

'Leave it with me.' He cut the connection and she crouched down again to check on the girl.

Her struggle for breath was increasing the blueness of her lips and extremities, and when Tammy checked her pulse she was seriously concerned. She tried to reassure the girl. Seeing her doing nothing, Jake stood up and asked, 'Can we go home now, Mummy?'

'In a minute, when someone else comes to help.'

Several passers-by had looked at them curiously but had given them a wide berth so Tammy offered up a prayer of thanks when she saw Ben running across the hospital grounds toward them. He was carrying a portable oxygen supply and Tammy took it from him. Turning on the oxygen, she slipped the mask over the girl's face.

'Oxygen,' she explained, 'to help your breathing.'

The young girl gratefully clasped the mask to her face.

'How is she?' Ben gasped, trying to get his breath.

'Deteriorating. Pulse racing.'

'Resus ambulance just coming. No inhalers?'

'Empty.'

His answering expression showed his feelings at such irresponsibility. 'What's her name?'

'No idea. She's too breathless to tell me. I didn't want to root further through her bag without a witness.'

He nodded. 'Try now.'

Tammy took out a diary and opened it at the page of personal details. 'Melissa Thoms?' She looked towards the girl who nodded her confirmation.

An ambulance came through the hospital gates and, after checking with Tammy that there was no likelihood of injury, the paramedics transferred Melissa swiftly into the ambulance. Ben followed.

Tammy grasped Jake's hand and pulled him into a warm hug. 'Sorry about that, Jake, but she needed help.'

'Is that what you do every day?'

'Sometimes. I help in lots of different ways.'

She wanted to set off home, get Jake as far away from the scene as she could, but Ben was still working on the girl with the ambulance door open.

She hovered for a few moments longer and when Ben straightened up to look at the monitor she told him, 'If you don't need me any more, I'll take Jake home.'

'You've done enough,' he said as he turned. 'She's stabilising already.' Then, noticing the child who was dancing up and down and tugging at her hand, he said, 'Is that your son?'

She nodded and turned to go, but not before Ben had moved to the back of the vehicle to shut the back door and taken a closer look at them both.

'Oh, no!' he exclaimed. 'He's... I never imagined... I wouldn't have believed...' He shook his head and with an air of finality shut the door as the ambulance moved slowly off.

'Can we go home now that a proper doctor is looking after her?' Jake was tugging relentlessly at her arm.

Furious with herself for caring that when Ben had taken on board the presence of her son he had revealed he wasn't so keen on children after all, she cuddled Jake to her side and said, 'Of course we can, love. The sooner we get as far away from here, the better.'

Until that moment Ben clearly hadn't thought about the responsibility having a child involved.

CHAPTER FIVE

TAMMY'S mind was working overtime as Jake set off as
fast as his little legs could manage, pulling her along with
him. However, she tried not to let him see how Ben's reaction to him had dismayed her. Instead, she laughed and
said, 'I bet you're ready for that biscuit I promised. So am
I.'

The moment they were indoors, she filled the kettle and
switched it on, then poured Jake a drink of milk and opened
a pack of chocolate biscuits.

'I think we deserve a treat after having some work to do
on my day off, don't you?'

Jake nodded solemnly. 'I 'serve one, too? I was a good
boy, wasn't I?'

She hugged him warmly. 'You certainly were.'

'So I can have a treat as well?'

'Of course you can.' Apart from not thinking of her as
a proper doctor, Tammy wondered what else he was thinking about the incident with Melissa. But after finishing his
milk and biscuit in silence, he wandered off into the playroom to play with his talking railway engine.

She took her coffee through and sat down to watch. He
chattered to her about Thomas and the other engines and
then brought a book of one of their adventures for her to
read.

She knew that he hadn't forgotten the events of the
morning but would probably not talk about what happened
until he was ready to do so. That was what usually happened and she knew from experience it was pointless to try
to hurry the process.

The story finished, he returned to his engines, giving Tammy time for her own thoughts. And shattering ones they were.

Not about Melissa. She was pretty sure the girl would be fine once the drugs took effect. No. It had been the shock on Ben's face as he'd uttered those words when seeing Jake for the first time.

Although she had been completely honest with him, he obviously hadn't taken on board the enormity of her life as the mother of a four-year-old. Now he had, it was obvious he was no different to every other eligible man she had met since Jazz had died. Scared she might be looking for someone to share the responsibility.

But this time it hurt as it never had in the past. She had valued Ben's friendship and had been pleased when he'd said he'd like to meet Jake. His few words at the door of the ambulance had changed all that.

'Mummy?'

'Yes, love?' Tammy shook herself free from her misery and immersed herself in the needs of her son.

'Can we have some lunch?'

'Already?' she asked with surprise, as it was only half past eleven. But then she remembered he'd been up at five-thirty.

'Yes, please. Can we have the lasagne that was left over from yesterday?'

'If I can find it, you certainly can.'

He rushed through to the kitchen, opened the fridge door and pointed to it triumphantly. 'There it is, Mummy.'

As she took it out to warm through, Tammy thought again what a treasure Lauren was. She not only loved Jake as if he were her own, she was an excellent cook. Tammy dreaded the day she might decide to marry and have a family of her own. Or even feel she wanted a change of scenery. For that reason she had always paid Lauren above the going rate and treated her like one of the family.

After his early morning, Jake was exhausted by teatime and Tammy was about to suggest he go upstairs for a leisurely bathtime when there was a knock on the door.

Frowning, she peered through the peephole and saw Ben standing there.

She pulled open the door and demanded, 'What are you doing here? You're on call.'

'Can I come in out of this rain?' he pleaded. 'Then I'll explain.'

When she stood back he shook himself like a dog, then joined her in the hall. 'I wanted to check that Jake was all right after the excitement this morning.'

'Excitement? Oh! You mean the asthmatic girl. Yes. He's fine, thanks.' Her response was cool as she remembered his remarks at the door of the ambulance. 'But shouldn't you be at the hospital?'

'George is covering for me for a couple of hours.'

'Why?'

He frowned. 'Because I wanted to see you were both OK.'

'Why?' she demanded, unbending in defence of her son.

'I thought we were friends.'

At that moment Jake came racing down the hall to see who was there and to tell his mother, 'Come and see what I've done with my track. The engine goes right r-round.' He stumbled over the last word as he caught sight of Ben. 'I saw you 's morning.'

'Hello, Jake. Yes, you did see me but I didn't have time to say hello then. I'm Ben.' He held a hand which Jake solemnly shook. 'I love railways. Can I see yours?'

Jake nodded eagerly and raced back into the playroom. 'I've put in a level-crossing there and changed the points to the other side. The engine runs right round now.' Jake set the engine down on the track.

Ben had followed him down onto the floor. 'That's a fantastic layout you've built,' he told the boy, who went on to explain the reasoning behind it.

A surprised Tammy watched as Ben chatted to Jake for nearly an hour about the various engines and the layout. She tried to puzzle out why he was there. Did he regret his earlier reaction to Jake? Certainly it seemed hard now to believe.

When he eventually clambered to his feet, Tammy said, 'I think it's long past your bedtime, young man. You were up early this morning.'

Jake started to grizzle.

Ben got to his feet. 'Would you like me to take you up?'

'Yes! Yes! Yes! You can stay here, Mummy. Ben'll take me.'

Ben gave her a rueful glance. 'Mummy can come, too.'

'No, I want you to take me and to read to me. You know about railways. Mummy doesn't.'

'Sorry,' he murmured. 'I was trying to help.'

'But what about the hospital? Shouldn't you—?'

'George'll cope.' He lifted Jake over his shoulder and followed his directions to the bathroom.

Tammy watched helplessly. 'If you really *don't* mind.'

She followed Ben up the stairs and watched while Jake washed and cleaned his teeth and clambered into his pyjamas.

'Just one story, Jake. Dr Davey has to get back to the hospital.'

'He's called Ben, Mum.'

Tammy smiled and made her way downstairs. As she cleared up the toys from the floor of the playroom, she could hear excited footsteps and shrieking for the next few minutes and then all went quiet. Curious, she crept back up the stairs and saw Ben sitting on the floor by Jake's bed, reading a story from the large tank engine book.

It was nearly half an hour later that he called her in to say goodnight. Jake was nearly asleep and she kissed him then indicated to Ben they should go back downstairs.

'That was good of you, Ben. He—'

'I didn't intend to monopolise his bedtime.' Ben looked anxious.

She shrugged. 'It gave me a break, but what about…?'

He checked his watch. 'The hospital can wait a few more minutes. I have my mobile.' While he spoke he looked around the room.

'Have you lost something, Ben?'

He shook his head. 'I was wondering, you have no photographs of Jake's father?'

'Not on display.'

He frowned. 'Why's that?'

She didn't answer, but the look on her face was glacial. He said gently, 'I'm sorry, Tammy. Perhaps you don't have any.'

She didn't move for a long moment and then nodded. 'I have a few. I'm keeping them to show Jake when he's older.'

Not for herself? 'I'd love to see some of them. Would that be possible? I'm just curious to see if Jake gets his looks from the paternal side or…'

She gave a deep sigh that filled him with remorse.

He moved over onto the arm of the chair she was sitting in and slid an arm gently around her shoulders. 'I'm sorry, Tammy. If it's going to upset you, forget I asked.'

She shook her head. 'No. I'll get them.'

She reached into the corner bookcase and pulled out a sizeable album and started to turn over the pages. 'That was Jazz when I first met him.' She pointed to a colour photograph of a brooding young man on a beach.

Ben felt as though he'd been punched in the stomach and found himself unable to speak immediately. He gasped in a lungful of air. It was James. There could be no mistake. He'd taken that photograph himself just before James had left home. He'd sent him a copy and James must have given it to Tammy.

He withdrew his arm to look more closely at the photograph, and then realised tears were pouring down her face.

'Tammy, I'm so sorry. I'm being very thoughtless. I think I ought to level with you. After I saw Jake this morning I was pretty sure I knew who his father was. That's why I had to come and check.' He quickly pulled her towards him and, holding her close, dabbed at the tears with a tissue from the box on the coffee-table. 'That photo is of my cousin, James. In fact, I took it. Jake is so like my cousin as a boy that I was almost certain they were related. And that proves it.'

She gulped in an effort to stem the tears, too overwrought for the implications of all he was saying to sink in. When they did, she gave a breathless shudder and sank back into her chair, pushing away his attempt to comfort her.

To give her time to come to terms with the enormity of the situation, he flipped over the next couple of pages of the album and uttered a gasp of amazement. One of the snaps there showed James holding a large canvas of a landscape. He groaned and dropped his head into his hands.

The truth slotted into place like the pieces of a jigsaw. When he'd left home James had obviously studied art. As he'd always wanted.

Ben had admired a painting by a painter named Jazz when he'd been viewing a house that had been for sale, but he'd had no idea his cousin had painted it. He'd already decided against the house, but had been intrigued by the painting. The owner had told him the name of the artist but that the price of his work was spiralling because Jazz had died tragically young.

He groaned. Jake's father *was* dead. James was dead. He would never see his cousin again. He swallowed hard. 'I can hardly take it in, Tammy.' His voice was barely a whisper. 'How am I going to tell his mother he'll never come home…?'

Tammy shook her head and closed the album with an air of finality, then tentatively rested her hand lightly on his arm, wanting to comfort him but not invade his private grief with her own distress.

He gathered her gently into his arms and murmured, 'This is all so surreal…'

Cradling her to him as much for his sake as hers, he wiped the tears from her cheeks with his thumb and whispered, 'He was a lucky man to be so loved.'

She didn't answer and he felt violent sobs accompanying the tears coursing down her cheeks in a rivulet.

'No, don't think that, Ben,' she sniffed. 'You've got it wrong. I didn't love him.' Overwrought by the see-sawing of her emotions since early that morning when she'd thought Ben had been horrified at the sight of Jake prancing about at her side, her sobs were becoming uncontrollable.

'Tammy, don't reproach yourself this way. It's a common reaction to the death of a loved one to feel guilty that you haven't done enough for them.' He hugged her to him and when she became even more distressed he whispered, 'Don't, Tammy. It's obvious how much you must have loved him and Jake is the tangible evidence of that.'

'No. No. *No.* It's not what you think, Ben. I didn't love him. Couldn't. By the time he died, I couldn't—' She broke off suddenly as she realised what she'd been about to blurt out. When Jake had been born she had vowed he would never know what his father had really been like and for that reason she couldn't share the truth with anyone. Not even her parents.

'I don't understand…'

She knew she couldn't tell Ben the whole story because Jazz had been his cousin—more like a brother, he'd called him—and that thought upset her more than ever. Somehow she had to impress on him that he must forget what she had said so far and never breathe a word of it to anyone.

'Ben, I—I can't explain. No one was ever meant to know. I want Jake to be proud of his father and if anyone, including my mother, finds out…'

He pulled her down beside him on the settee. 'Tammy, it sounds to me as if you need to talk—and I'm a good person to talk to. I'm a doctor and bound by the Hippocratic oath. I won't repeat what I hear to Jake or anyone else for that matter,' he said gently.

He handed her another fistful of tissues and she scrubbed at her eyes. 'I can't… I've bottled it up for so long…'

'Then it's time you removed the stopper. Let me get you a drink. And then we can settle to chat.'

She dabbed at her eyes. 'You have to get back to the hospital.'

'Forget the hospital. Remember, *I* have quiet shifts.' She acknowledged his joke with a weak smile as he went on, 'It was all quiet when I came away and George will ring me if he's stretched. Now, that drink?'

'A glass of water would be lovely. What about you?'

'Water's fine for me, too.'

She heard him opening one cupboard after another, but eventually he returned with two tumblers of cold water.

'Right. I'm all ears.'

Aware he was attempting to lighten a difficult time for her, she tried to acknowledge his quip with a watery smile. 'Thanks, Ben.'

She downed a couple of sips of the water and then, shaking her head, said, 'This is impossible, Ben. When Jazz died I vowed for Jake's sake never to tell anyone…'

'I'm not anyone.'

When she didn't continue, he encouraged her with a reassuring touch on the back of her hand. 'Take your time.'

'I meant what I said. I no longer loved Jazz when he died,' she blurted out. 'You—you had that so wrong.' She took a deep breath. 'My tears were not because I loved him. Just the opposite.'

She shook her head. 'Ben, I couldn't bear it if Jake found out that his father was less than perfect.'

'He won't. But I think you need to remember that none of us are perfect.' He held her close, his hand gently caressing.

'I'm sorry, Ben, so sorry. You're the last person I can tell this to. He was your cousin.'

He sealed her lips with a forefinger. 'If it helps, I can tell you that nothing you tell me about James will surprise me. I probably know his faults better than you.' He cradled her in his arms until the tremors that were shaking her body began to subside. 'When did you realise what he was like?'

'Soon after I moved in. I discovered he hadn't paid the money he'd collected on the Paris trip into the rag fund, and when I asked him about it he…'

'He what, Tammy?' Ben prompted. She couldn't say anything for some time because her sobs came thick and fast until she burst out, 'I— That was probably the night Jake was conceived. You see…' She hiccoughed, searching for words. 'He's not a reminder of our love at all.'

'You mean he made love to you to avoid telling you the truth. That he'd spent it, probably,' Ben muttered darkly. 'Why am I not surprised?'

'I really thought he cared until…' She caught her breath before finishing in a rush, 'Until I told him I was pregnant. I thought he'd be as pleased as I was. Instead, he made it clear that I meant nothing to him and never had—he said I was just a meal ticket—so I would have to get rid of the baby. He was killed in a car accident the next day. And I was glad.' She shuddered violently and a low, tortured sound escaped from her lips.

Ben tightened his hold and shook his head. 'I don't think anyone would blame you for that. I'm disgusted, Tam, for the hell a relative of mine has put you through.'

'I knew I shouldn't have told you.'

'I think I'm probably the best person,' he said softly, 'because I know—knew him so well, I have no difficulty believing it.'

When she started to quieten, he tipped her head up slightly so that he could see her face. Then he leaned forward and kissed her lips so gently that if her eyelids hadn't flickered open, she wouldn't have been sure.

'I'm so sorry, Tammy. I knew he was selfish, but…' He sank back onto the chair behind him and dropped his head into his cupped hands and she sensed his anguish. 'And I'll have to tell my aunt—'

'*No!* You promised.'

Ben shook his head. 'I'll only tell her that he's dead. Nothing more.'

'I've made it difficult for you. I shouldn't have—'

'Told me? Of course you should. You needed to. And I needed to know.'

She smiled wanly, grateful for his attempt to reassure her. 'Your aunt is going to be devastated—her only son,' Tammy whispered. 'I suppose I should call her Jake's grandmother now.' She shook her head as if trying to wake from a nightmare. 'Jake's grandmother? That's going to take a bit of getting used to—for all of us.'

'Jake's related to me. I think I rather like that idea,' he told her as he hugged her close, and this time his kiss wasn't so light and gentle.

Ben's mobile rang out in the quiet room and he swore and moved to the other side of the room to answer it. After a prolonged conversation he finished the call and walked back to take Tammy's hand ruefully.

'I'm so sorry, Tammy. That was George—I'm going to have to go. And work is the last thing I want to think about at the moment.'

Tight-lipped, Tammy nodded. 'I'm so sorry, Ben. Hell, I've ruined your memories of James for ever.'

'Not really. He was spoilt and immature but I always thought he would grow up one day and regret his behaviour. And he can't let me down now, can he?'

She shook her head in wonderment at him finding such a compassionate way to reassure her.

'No. It's you I'm worried about. Now, are you going to be all right here, or would you like—?'

'I just need to be on my own. And thanks, Ben.'

'What for?'

'For giving me a chance to unburden myself and for being so—so understanding.'

He searched her face and whispered, 'Take care of yourself, Tammy, *and* that wonderful son of yours.'

When she started to move, he restrained her gently. 'Stay there, I'll see myself out.'

He kissed her cheek and was gone.

Tammy remained seated as he made his way to the front door. The moment it closed behind him, she flung herself down onto the settee and wept.

What had she done? Jazz was Ben's cousin, for goodness' sake. How stupid could she be? What on earth had possessed her to confide in him?

And how on earth was she going to face him on Monday, let alone the time they'd be working together? She was so ashamed of what she'd told him that she couldn't sleep for wondering if they could ever work together again.

What a stupid fool she'd been to allow her emotions to overwhelm her usual caution. Until now she'd kept her secret with no difficulty. What had changed?

It could only be Ben. Her colleague and her friend, Jazz's cousin! She felt a fierce heat suffuse her cheeks at the thought of what she'd done to him. She had liked him and had been touched by the way he had related to Jake. But now—now she had probably alienated him for ever, despite his attempt at reassurance. And that was typical of him. He must have been devastated by her revelation, and yet he sought only to make things easier for her.

Her repeated tearful self-recrimination meant she barely slept that night, and Sunday passed slowly as she wondered whether to ruin her career by breaking her contract or to brazen it out when she met him as if nothing untoward had taken place.

Her thoughts weren't helped by Jake repeatedly asking when Ben would come and see them again. Especially when she didn't hear from him apart from a curt message asking if she was OK on the answering-machine when she and Jake returned from the morning church service.

She tried to ring him back a few times, but he was always busy or on another line. When she hadn't heard from him by mid-afternoon she knew she really *had* blown any hope of a continuing friendship. The kindest thing she could do was to let him know she understood. So she rang the hospital again and left a message that she was fine, and as she was going to visit her mother for the rest of the day she would see him on Monday.

For Jake's sake she tried to push her worries to the back of her mind, but when Monday morning came she wasn't looking forward to returning to the hospital and facing Ben.

Lauren had arrived home extremely late on Sunday evening and Tammy was loath to wake her when it was time to leave. However, she staggered from her room when she heard Jake running around the landing.

He flung his arms around Lauren, making Tammy momentarily jealous. Why couldn't she stay and be hugged like that? Then reason kicked in and she kissed him goodbye and set off down the stairs.

Lauren followed her to the door. 'No problems?'

Tammy shook her head. 'And your lasagne was fantastic.'

'You're on call tonight?'

Tammy nodded. ''Fraid so. See you tomorrow,' she called up to Jake, and felt tears well in her eyes as she made her way to her car.

Snap out of it, she told herself firmly. You love your work and you know he's fine. And he'll soon start school and then what would you do with your time?

Ben was sitting at the desk in the office when she arrived on the ward. 'Hi.'

'Much changed this weekend?' she asked, as she studied the hand-over report to avoid looking at him.

'As you know, apart from Melissa, Saturday was quiet. Yesterday made up for it.'

'Your turn for the busy shift at last. How is Melissa?'

'She's much better. She responded to the nebulised drugs very quickly—in fact, she was already improving with the oxygen and your care. However, we did admit her. Unfortunately there were no paediatric beds so she's on the female ward.'

'How old is she?'

'Barely fifteen. Old enough to take responsibility for her own treatment, though. What's much more important, Tammy, are *you* all right?

She ignored the question. 'Is Melissa one of our previous patients?'

He sighed and shook his head. 'She wasn't but the

asthma team will keep an eye on her from now on. She's been treated by her GP who seems to have done all the right things, but her mother says she tries to pretend the asthma doesn't exist and ignores everything he says. I imagine he hasn't the time to check up on her.'

'What about his nurse? Doesn't she run an asthma clinic?'

'Tammy, we need to talk…'

Determined to behave as if nothing had happened, she retorted, 'We are talking.'

'Not about the things that matter.'

'Don't the patients matter?'

'You know what I mean.'

'So doesn't Melissa's nurse run an asthma clinic?'

He sighed and with obvious exasperation replied. 'Her mother didn't mention one.'

Tammy wrinkled her nose. 'Pity. Melissa probably hates to appear different to her peers and so needs the message constantly reinforced.'

'You don't have to tell me. The number of asthmatic youngsters dying unnecessarily, especially girls, is spiralling. The treatment that's available should mean we get no deaths. None at all.'

'I'll try and pop along to see her and attempt to impress on her just how bad she was when I found her.' Her voice suddenly wavered as her memory of Saturday was triggered.

'You're not all right, are you, Tam?'

'I'm fine, thanks. But I ought to get on or I won't be ready for the ward round.'

Ben wasn't going to let her escape so easily. 'There's no rush. Mike and I are doing the round on the female side first today. Tammy,' he said gently, 'we can't pretend Saturday evening never happened. We do need to talk more about the situation. Perhaps we could have a chat over a late coffee or lunch.'

She shrugged. 'I don't think we have anything more to say to one another, Ben.' She set off out of the office.

'If you're taking a look at the patients, I'll come with you. I can update you on everything that's happened over the weekend. Quicker and better than any charts.'

He led the way to the first bed. 'Mr Burt has improved greatly. I should think we can soon discharge him. These two are new admissions—Mr Knut and Bob Grant, two victims of a dratted bug that seems to be taking hold around here. They both have secondary chest infections and are already responding to treatment.'

She nodded. 'And Billy Old is slowly improving by the sound of it.'

'He is, yes, but I can't see his wife is ever going to manage him at home.'

'So what are you suggesting?'

'A transfer to the geriatric unit and, when one can be found, a bed in a nursing home.'

'Poor Billy.' She knew Ben was watching her anxiously and she dashed a hand across her eyes. Normally she would feel sadness for patients like Billy and his wife, but accept it was for the best. But today her own situation was making her over-empathise with her patients.

She strode on to the next bed. Ben briefed her on what was happening to the rest of the patients and then hurried off to join Mike on the female side.

Some fifteen minutes later they arrived together to take a look at the men.

Mike acknowledged her with a nod. The round was quite straightforward, apart from Mr Wood who wanted to go home. Mike could see no reason why he couldn't.

They all returned to the office to discuss a couple of

problems that had arisen, but when Jan brought in a tray of coffee Tammy rose to her feet and said, 'I must get on.'

She didn't see Ben again until she was eating her early lunch in the canteen with Jan.

Jan beckoned him across to join them. 'I didn't think you'd still be around.'

The question prompted him to yawn widely. 'I might have a short nap after the clinic but I can't claim it was a bad weekend.'

'I didn't mean sleeping. I thought you'd be off house-hunting again once the round was finished.' Jan laughed and explained, 'Did you know that every house he goes for the surveyor finds to have an insurmountable problem?'

Without looking up from her food, Tammy shook her head. 'Perhaps you should change the surveyor!'

'Perhaps I should.' He spoke ruefully. 'If it wasn't so time-consuming and expensive I'd get another survey done on this one in Park Road. It would be so convenient for the hospital.'

'Park Road?' Tammy frowned. 'I can't believe there's a problem with any house there.'

Ben raised an eyebrow. 'You know them?'

She nodded. 'I should do. My parents live at number twenty-seven. Have done since it was built. And I'm pretty sure the houses were all built around the same time, some thirty years ago.'

'Maybe, but number eighty-two has an extension with foundations this chap says are inadequate. He thinks the previous owner probably built it himself without anyone checking it. Maybe he didn't have planning permission.'

'Ah! That's different. I don't know that end of the road. Can't you ask him?'

He grinned. 'Difficult. I don't have a hotline to heaven.'

Tammy found herself colouring at her mistake and he

leaned across to rest a consoling hand on her arm. 'You weren't to know.'

Jan stood up. 'Can I get either of you a coffee?'

They both nodded and Ben handed over some change. 'My treat.' Then he whispered urgently to Tammy, 'You must accept we need to talk. Before I tell my aunt about her son I want to be armed with the whole story about his death.'

'You haven't told her about me yet?'

'No—I want to tell her face to face. As there's no immediate rush I think that's only fair.'

Tammy nodded and after a moment's thought she said, 'Jazz died in a car accident. I'll let you have all the newspaper reports. That will tell you everything you need to know.'

'She'll want to meet Jake.'

'I know. And I'll arrange it when that time comes.'

'I don't need this, Tammy.' His exclamation was anguished. 'And neither do you. I'd rather hear the details from you.'

'I don't want to talk about it any more.'

Exasperated, he returned to his food as Jan returned with their drinks.

She sat down, and after a moment said, 'Do I detect a distinct cooling of the atmosphere?' When neither of them answered, she said, 'Can't I leave you two alone for a moment?'

'Thanks for getting the coffees, Jan.' Ben drained his cup and noisily pushed his chair back. 'As I'm to blame, I'll leave you both to enjoy the rest of your break.'

They both watched until he'd disappeared through the canteen door, then Jan leaned excitedly towards Tammy. 'What was all that about? Come on. Spill.'

Tammy shrugged. 'I had my son with me when I found Melissa. Ben was asking about him.'

Jan turned to her eagerly. 'You have a son? I'd no idea. Does his father look after him while you're at work?'

'His father's dead.'

Jan rested a hand on Tammy's arm. 'That must be hard for you.'

'Not really. I have a brilliant nanny and I love my work, which I must now get back to, I suppose, but first I must check all's well at home.'

'Ah. That's who you ring so regularly.' Delight at solving the problem showed clearly on her face. 'I must say I have wondered. Why on earth didn't you say?'

Tammy shrugged. 'I try to keep the two sides of my life separate. But Ben seems to think I should talk about it and I don't want to. See you in a few minutes.' She made her way outside to make her call.

'What are you like, Benjamin Davey?' Jan found Ben in the office on her return.

'Me...er, what?'

'Hasn't that poor girl enough to cope with without you making matters worse?'

'Who—?'

'Don't give me that. You know who I'm talking about. The best junior doctor we've had on the ward since this place opened.'

'Jan, I don't think—'

'Well, I do. And if you don't apologise to her at once, I won't be answerable for my actions.'

'This is between Tammy and me, Jan.'

'Well, just you sort it. And the sooner, the better.'

Tammy came into the office to collect some notes. 'Mr Burt is not looking too good again,' she told Ben. 'I need to chase up this morning's blood-test results.'

Ben frowned at her impersonal tone as she picked up the telephone and dialled the number, then shrugged. 'I'll take a quick look at him.'

CHAPTER SIX

As TAMMY finished writing down the results, the crash bell warned of a cardiac arrest. She rushed into the ward and saw Jan drawing the curtains around Mr Burt's bed space and removing the pillows. Ben was clearing the patient's airway while checking his carotid pulse. He shook his head. 'No response to the chest thump.' A health-care assistant raced in with the crash trolley as Tammy and Jan struggled to remove the bedhead. Jan immediately switched to administering oxygen with a hand-held squeeze bag while Ben administered chest compressions. Tammy started to fill syringes with the drugs that might be necessary.

It seemed like long minutes but could only have been seconds before the hospital crash team arrived and took control.

'Carry on for the moment, Ben.' The anaesthetist checked the defibrillator, applied the paddles and then warned everyone to stand back. The trace on the monitor changed and he nodded. 'That looks encouraging. Keep an eye on the screen, Ben, and be ready to restart the compressions if necessary.'

'Do you want another line?' Tammy asked.

'We'll use his infusion for now, thanks.' He checked the drugs Tammy had prepared. 'I'll keep those to hand for the moment and ask John B. for his opinion.'

Tammy was relieved to know that he was going to involve the cardiac registrar, especially as she knew Ben would be in the outpatient clinic all afternoon.

When John and his registrar had arrived and taken control, Ben indicated that Tammy should join him in the office. 'Mike and I can cope with the outpatients until Mr Burt can be safely left.' He moved towards her with a frown. 'Are you all right, Tammy?'

'Of course.'

'Tammy...' He reached for her hand but she turned quickly on her heel and made her way back into the ward.

It was nearly an hour later when John left and Mr Burt's condition was sufficiently stable for Tammy to feel it was safe to remove the last of the paraphernalia that had arrived when he'd arrested and join Ben in the outpatient clinic.

He welcomed her with an unexpectedly warm smile. 'Mr Burt OK?'

'His wife's just come in and she says she thinks he looks better than he did yesterday!'

'Actually, we were very lucky it reverted so quickly. Now, do you think you could see these two follow-ups, Tammy? I think Mike and I can manage apart from that.'

She took the notes and as she made her way to the room allocated to her, she flicked through them and was pleased to see that Percy Good was one of them and had actually turned up. She wondered how he'd been persuaded to attend but it would be good to see how he was coping at home.

'Hello, Mr Good,' she greeted him. 'How are you?'

'OK.'

'How's your chest been since you've been at home?'

'OK.' He looked towards the door as if wondering whether he could escape now.

'Would you like to go through here and I'll listen to your chest?'

He moved reluctantly into the examination room and she waited while he removed his shirt.

'That sounds much better,' she said after checking him. 'You're not back at work yet, are you?'

'Started back Friday.'

'You use all the personal protective equipment your employers provide, do you?'

'Don't need any. They've found me a job in the stores.'

'And do you enjoy that?'

''S fine.'

She was getting nowhere with him. He'd made up his mind that he still didn't trust them and there was nothing she could do about it. It certainly seemed, though, that the personnel department were bending over backwards to accommodate Percy, so perhaps there was something in what Ben had said.

'Have you been to see your GP?'

'No need.'

'What about your repeat prescriptions?'

'The chemist picks them up.'

'And your doctor hasn't asked to see you?'

'He's asked, but I haven't had the time.'

'He won't keep on issuing your prescriptions without checking they are still what's needed.'

'I'll think about that when it happens.'

Tammy sighed. 'In the meantime, you'd better come back and see us here. Two months all right?'

He nodded and rushed off before she could suggest anything else.

She wrote up her findings in Percy's notes and called her next patient in. It was John Lowe, who had been her first patient when she'd started on Clarke Ward.

'I'm fine now,' he told her. 'Never had anything like that before and never want it again.'

'I'd just like to check you over before we sign you off.'

When he left, there were a couple of other follow-up patients for her to see, then she was called back to the ward to talk with Mr Wood's wife, who'd arrived to take him home and took a lot of convincing that he did not have lung cancer.

Ben joined her on the ward when the clinic finished, later than usual. He looked tired and dejected.

'You're on call, aren't you?'

She nodded.

'Mike's admitting that last new patient He's coming to us via X-Ray.'

'What's the problem?'

'It would probably be easier to list what he doesn't have wrong with him. Heart failure, bronchitis, emphysema and maybe even a touch of pneumonia. I'll stay and see what we can do to make him more comfortable this evening and start ordering the various tests Mike suggests we do.'

'I can do that. You've been on call since Friday.'

'I'll survive.' He yawned. 'See what you've done now. I hadn't thought about being tired until you mentioned it.'

'I'll try and find you a cup of coffee.' She needed to escape and set off towards the door, but he caught her arm and said, 'Not for a minute, Tammy. It's so difficult to get even a moment alone with you.'

'Ben, I—'

'I know—you want to pretend Saturday never happened. But it did and I'm glad. For both of us.'

She looked up at him. 'But when I didn't hear from you on Sunday, I thought—'

'I really *was* busy on Sunday, Tammy. I wasn't trying to avoid speaking to you.'

'Even though you had good reason…'

'I'm not Jazz, Tammy,' he told her gently. 'I might be his cousin but I'm a very different person.'

She nodded. 'I realise that, but—'

'I'm a man. And not to be trusted? Tammy, you can't go through life not trusting any man because Jazz let you down.'

'I don't, well, perhaps occasionally…'

Ben grasped her shoulders and turned her to face him. 'Just when it's your happiness at stake?'

She couldn't answer because she knew he was right.

'Learning to trust again takes time—but I'm having to do it after Deanna so perhaps we could work at it together. What do you think?'

He imbued the seductive tone he was using with such a comic pleading that she could do nothing but grin and say, 'I'll try.'

'That's settled, then. Now, how is Jake?'

'Fine.' Tammy tried to be diffident, but couldn't resist adding, 'He keeps asking when you're going to visit again.'

Heedless of where they were, he hugged her with more ferocity than a bear could have done. 'Dear girl, don't you realise those are the sweetest words I've heard all day. I'd *love* to visit him again.'

Struggling to free herself before he could realise just how the close contact of their bodies was affecting her, Tammy murmured, 'I suppose we're both off next weekend—some time then perhaps?'

'That would be absolutely wonderful. Let's make it Saturday. I intend to visit my aunt during the morning so perhaps around teatime.'

As he spoke, Mr Dennis arrived from X-Ray, so they had no further opportunity to chat about anything but the patients. But later that evening, when everything had quietened down on the ward and Tammy had time to think as she lay sleepless on the narrow bed, she couldn't help wondering if Jake was Ben's only reason for wanting to visit.

Had his suggestion that they work together at overcoming their lack of trust a deeper meaning than she'd first thought? Deanna not wanting children had obviously hurt him deeply. She'd told him that she'd been determined to have Jake, whatever his cousin had said, so she obviously cared about children. Did that make her an attractive proposition?

Whatever, denying him contact with Jake would be cruel. Especially when Jake liked him as much as she did. That thought startled her wide awake. How much did she like him? And how much did she trust him? Her answer to both surprised her, especially when she didn't want any involvement in the near future—or ever if he was only attracted to her because of her maternal qualities.

It was a relief to escape such tortuous thoughts when she was called to the ward to see Stan Burt. He was causing them all a lot of concern. His heavy exposure to asbestos had resulted in asbestosis so severe that there was not a lot they could do for him but make him comfortable.

Despite his breathlessness and the discomfort he was suffering, he never grumbled, and Mr Dennis and Mr Knut, who were both improving, did everything they could to make life easier for him.

The three men were a troublesome trio in the friendliest possible way. They'd known one another slightly when they'd been admitted and now they had formed a gang that teased the nurses and Tammy unmercifully. It wasn't long before they got an inkling that there was an undercurrent between Tammy and Ben.

That made life difficult when she was so unsure herself about Ben, and more than once they embarrassed her by comments made in his presence.

When Tammy joined Jan for lunch on Friday, she was exhausted. 'I don't think I've ever known a week like this.'

Jan agreed. 'This latest bug doing the rounds seems to be picking on those with weak chests.'

'I suppose the healthy among us can fight it off. The origins of this one seem to be a mystery as well. I was reading a piece in my journal only last night. Apparently it's now affecting young babies. Thank goodness Jake is past that stage. I'd have been scared in case I was taking it home to him.'

Jan nodded. 'It's not until they are born that we realise how many things could go wrong with them.'

'I know. I always seem to be worrying about him for one reason or another. Does it get easier when they reach their teens, Jan?'

She laughed. 'No. If anything, it gets worse.'

'That's a great consolation, thanks.'

'Always glad to be useful.' Jan's glib answer made Tammy smile wryly. 'Anything else I can help you with? Like pushing you and Ben Davey into one another's arms?'

Tammy grimaced. 'Don't even think things like that, Jan, let alone say them.'

'Why not? You are both available and even the patients have noticed you seem to be getting on much better this week. I think he's just what you need.'

'I'm not ready for a relationship and, anyway, I can tell you from experience that most single men run a mile from a ready-made family.'

'Not Ben. He's been over to Sunday lunch with us a couple of times and he's wonderful with the kids. Got family man stamped right through him—like a stick of rock. If you get my drift!'

'Jan!' Tammy pretended to be scandalised.

Her colleague hooted with laughter. 'That *was* an unfortunate analogy, wasn't it? But you know what I mean.'

Tammy nodded. 'Even so, I'm sure he would prefer any family to be his own. So, please, promise you'll forget any matchmaking schemes you might be hatching.'

As she walked back to the ward Tammy thought about what Jan had said and knew she was right. That was no doubt why she herself had felt so attracted to him. He was a caring and considerate man. Any child would be lucky to have him as a father and, she admitted ruefully to herself, any wife would be looked after and cared for in a way she never had been by Jazz. What an immature fool she'd been to be taken in by such a shallow man when, if she'd waited, there were others like Ben just around the corner.

Not that she regretted Jake's birth for one moment. He was the most important person in the world to her and she loved him dearly.

After spending most of Saturday with his aunt, Ben tried to push the horror of it to the back of his mind and concentrate on enjoying the next couple of hours with Jake and Tammy. But his aunt had raised questions in his mind that refused to be denied.

She had demanded to know why Tammy was neglecting her son to go to work if Jazz's paintings were selling so well. It was fair comment and not for the first time Ben regretted having had to leave Tammy the previous Saturday evening without discovering all the details surrounding her relationship with his late cousin.

Was Tammy delegating the care of her child because her career was more important to her? He'd been down that road once and didn't want to traverse it again, but he couldn't believe Tammy felt that way. She obviously loved the time she spent with Jake and general practice had many more opportunities for shorter hours than hospital medicine.

It was a few minutes after five when he knocked on Tammy's door. Her smile of welcome was warm and he couldn't resist kissing her cheek lightly before handing over the flowers he was carrying.

'How lovely.' She breathed in the scent of the bouquet and said, 'The freesias are gorgeous.'

He could smell nothing but *her* heady perfume. It assailed his nostrils when he dropped a chaste kiss on her cheek, arousing such a storm of desire within him that he quickly held out another parcel. 'This is for Jake. A jigsaw puzzle. If that's all right?'

'Take it through. He's in the garden. He won't have heard you as you didn't ring the bell.'

Ben made his way through the kitchen where a mouth-watering spread was already prepared.

'Jake,' Tammy called from behind his shoulder. 'Ben is here.'

The boy turned and greeted him with James's smile and flung his arm round Ben's neck, swinging his feet off the floor as he did so.

'Careful, Jake,' Tammy admonished. 'Don't hurt Ben.'

The boy released his hold and, his heart aching for Jake's need of a father figure, Ben handed him the parcel. 'I thought you might like this.'

The boy tore at the paper eagerly to reveal a picture of a train. One of the tank engine's friends. 'Gosh. Percy. Thank you. I haven't got that one. I'm glad I made you chocolate cakes for tea.'

He heard Tammy giggle and turned towards her with an indulgent wink.

'Come through and have tea,' she said quickly. 'It just needs to be carried to the table. Jake! Come and wash your hands.'

Jake placed the puzzle carefully on the coffee-table before going out to do as his mother had ordered.

'Can I help with the carrying?' Ben followed Tammy into the kitchen.

She handed him a couple of dishes and then a couple of plates. 'We can start when Jake gets back. Would you like tea? Or coffee?'

'Whatever.'

She brought a pot of tea through and set it at the far end of the table. Jake climbed up on the cushions that had obviously been placed on the chair for him and said to Ben, 'I want you to sit by me.'

Ben did as he was told and found it meant he was kept busy answering the boy's questions or keeping him supplied with food.

'Can I have more ham, Mummy?'

She nodded. 'One more piece, then you must eat your bread and salad and let Ben eat his.'

'I like bread and ham, don't you, Ben?' Jake was trying hard to sound grown-up and they both tried to hide their amusement at the incongruity.

'I do hope you managed to eat enough,' Tammy said after Ben had eaten and admired one of the chocolate buns Jake had made.

'Can I get down and do the puzzle now?'

'OK. But wash your hands first. I'll clear the table for you.'

'I'll help with the jigsaw, if you like. If that's all right?' Ben looked at Tammy for approval.

'Fine, but we must leave time for a bath tonight.'

'Perhaps we can talk after that.' Realising he was becoming too preoccupied with what he wanted to say to her, he said, 'I must say, he's a lovely boy, and so bright.'

'You mean he didn't allow you to get a word in edgeways?'

He grinned. 'We certainly haven't had a chance to say much to one another, have we?'

It was well past seven before Ben had read Jake three stories and the boy had agreed to snuggle under his duvet ready to sleep.

Ben sank into the chair opposite Tammy with a sigh of relief and she laughed. 'He's hard work, isn't he?'

'It must be harder when there's only one parent.'

She shrugged. 'Maybe. And maybe not. Depends how

supportive the other parent is…' She stopped in mid-sentence and hastily changed the subject.

She leaned across and rested a hand on his arm. 'Jazz told me he had no living relatives.' She looked up at him and traced a finger down his cheek. 'But I can see now why I thought I knew you on my first day at the General. There *is* a likeness. Quite definitely. I can't believe that I never made the connection.'

He caught her hand between his. 'You weren't looking for it. That's why. I was geared up to looking for James which meant Jake being so like him was obvious to me. If you'd told me Jazz was an artist I might have put two and two together much earlier.'

Tammy shrugged. 'I'd probably have done so if you hadn't been so scathing about artists when Klaus Rey was admitted.'

He recalled his annoyance that day and berated himself for it. 'Because I knew that was what James wanted to do when he left home, I suppose I transferred my fury at the hassle I was having with my aunt to Klaus.'

'I don't actually recall you telling me that your cousin rowed with his father because he wanted to become an artist either. If you had, I might have done the adding up, though I doubt it somehow.'

She was right. Come to think of it, he hadn't told her.

'How did your aunt react to the news? Was it awful?'

'I'm not sure if it really sank in. It certainly didn't at first. It took me a long time to convince her and when I did she wanted answers to a lot of questions. Some of which I couldn't answer. She was so unmoved that even when I left I felt she hadn't really accepted she would never see him again.'

'Do you think deep down she could have suspected the truth all along?'

'Maybe. Perhaps if she'd been able to mourn at the time

it would be easier. Seeing his death certificate in black and white might help, I suppose. I presume you still have it.'

'I do, but I knew him as Jazz Armstrong and that's the name on his certificate.'

She shuddered as she remembered the events surrounding his death. 'It wasn't an easy time, Ben.'

He crossed to sit on the arm of her chair and slid a comforting arm around her shoulders. 'I can imagine. I presume the change of name was to prevent anyone tracing his whereabouts.'

'I never found a birth certificate or any other form of identification and the university couldn't help either. Apparently he kept promising to take his birth certificate in and never did. The various authorities thought I was trying to pull a fast one, but I'd only known him a relatively short time. Eventually when they discovered he had no money, they decided it wasn't worth pursuing their enquiries and allowed me to arrange the funeral.'

Ben frowned. 'No money at all? What about car insurance for the accident?'

Tammy laughed mirthlessly. 'The car was neither taxed nor insured.'

Ben let out a quiet whistle and shook his head. 'And I suppose his pictures weren't selling at that time?'

'They were in a small way, but if he ever had any money from them he spent it right away.'

'I gather they've been in demand since he died.' Ben gratefully seized the opportunity to check out his aunt's allegations.

Stung by the hint of accusation she detected in his voice, she retorted, 'They have, but I didn't have that many. Quite a lot were destroyed in the accident, so most of the money has been made by people reselling them.'

'So you have to go out to work to keep the roof over your head?'

She gave a rueful nod.

Relieved to discover it was *necessary* for her to leave her child with the nanny, he said, 'I suppose you were still a student when he died?'

'In my final year.' She sucked in a lungful of air before saying, 'You think I'm living on money that is rightfully his mother's, don't you?'

His reply was anguished. 'No. I don't think that at all.'

'But your aunt does and you just had to make sure.'

'I told her you weren't that sort.'

But Tammy was so incensed that she wasn't listening. 'Don't forget his son's a next of kin as well. Even if he wasn't born at the time. You can tell her that I set up a small trust fund for Jake with money from the few pictures I did have, and it pays part of Lauren's wages—and that's all.'

She swivelled round in her chair, her arms wrapped tightly around her body. 'I think I'd like to be on my own now.'

'Tammy, the last thing I meant to do was upset you, but—'

'I know it can't have been an easy day for you and that you've probably talked about the situation ad nauseam with your aunt but, believe me, it's not exactly a picnic for me to discover that my son has numerous relatives on his paternal side that I don't know about but who are prepared to think the worst of me...' She buried her face in her hands.

'Don't, Tammy.' He raised her head with gentle hands and saw that her face was bleak. As bleak as it had been when she'd first told him about her son. But this time it was he that had caused it and not Jazz. He was growing to love Tammy and her son, but he hadn't been able to trust her because his aunt's repeated accusation about Tammy leaving her child to go to work had reminded him of his own unhappy childhood and the hurt Deanna had inflicted on him.

Reviling himself for his insensitivity, he folded his arms around her and said, 'I'm so sorry, love. So very sorry. It has been a difficult day but that's no excuse.'

She shrugged but remained silent.

'Tammy, I—'

'I'll find his death certificate and let you have it on Monday. I think we've said all that needs to be said for the moment.'

'Maybe. I guess this isn't easy for any of us.' He touched her cheek with his hand. When she didn't move, he pulled her closer. 'I'm so sorry.' He lowered his head slowly, almost hesitantly until their lips met, and he kissed her, softly at first, teasing and coaxing, until she pushed him away.

'Goodnight, Ben.'

'Goodnight, Tammy, and I'm so sorry.'

'You and me both,' she muttered as the door clicked shut behind him, leaving her alone and confused. She had wanted desperately to respond to him but it was obvious his aunt would never approve of Ben being involved with the villain of the piece who had lured her darling son away from his safe home. And that, coupled with the fact that Ben had just made it abundantly clear that he couldn't trust her, meant there could be no future for friendship or anything else between them, and that hurt.

And what was worse, she couldn't deny Jake contact with his grandmother now that she knew about her, so even when she moved on from her present job, Ben would still be in the background of Jake's family. Fate conspired to be very cruel at times.

Eventually she moved through to the kitchen and mechanically filled and switched on the kettle. Despite an early night, she didn't sleep until the early hours and even then her slumber was disturbed by dreams of Ben. Ben making love to her. Ben as part of their small family. Each time she awoke it was more difficult to shake off her dream-like belief that it was really happening. And when she did, the cold realisation came as a stark reminder of the impossibility of the situation.

Jake bouncing into her bedroom early the next morning, demanding to know if Ben was coming again soon, didn't help. Would she want to take responsibility for Ben's child if the situation were reversed? Of course she would. That was what made things even more unbearable. Men had a completely different view of these things.

It was just after nine when he rang and asked if she was OK.

'Yes.'

'How's Jake?'

'He's fine.'

'I'm on my way to visit my aunt this morning, but I wondered if we could meet up later. Perhaps I could take you and Jake out for Sunday lunch—'

'I'm sorry, Ben, we're lunching with my parents and we won't be home until late.'

'Could I take you out for something to eat this evening?'

'I'm not sure when Lauren will be back, and I've got a lot to do this evening. I'll see you tomorrow, Ben.'

To her relief she saw no sign of him before he arrived with Mike to do the ward round on Monday morning. She supposed they had come from the female side, having already done the round there.

To her relief there were no major problems with any of the patients, apart from Mike suggesting the time had come to transfer Billy from the acute ward.

Tammy grimaced. This was something she hadn't been looking forward to. 'I'll have a word with his wife and then see what I can organise.'

'It won't be easy, Tammy, but do your best. We really need to free up his bed for the acute cases.'

Ben didn't have a chance to talk to her alone until lunchtime when he followed her into the canteen.

'The ward round went well. No results missing.' It was obvious he was searching for something safe to say so she responded in the same vein.

'Seems to have been a quiet weekend as I wasn't on call.'

'Do you remember Melissa Thoms?' Tammy nodded. 'We discharged her this morning. Apparently she wasn't happy at school, but her parents have agreed to her going to the local college in the summer to do a child-care course. She's a different person. I don't think we'll have any more problems with her.'

'I'm glad to hear it.'

'A lot of that is down to you.'

Having paid for his food, he followed her to an empty table.

She concentrated on the salad she had chosen, but looked up when he said, 'Tammy, I really am sorry for what I said but we are both still learners at this trust thing, aren't we?'

She met his eyes as she said, 'Ben, I—I think this will only make an impossible situation worse.' She spoke hesitantly, aware that the wrong word here could make even working together impossible.

'I must say, Jake is a credit to you. You—you must be so proud of him.' He too was hesitant.

She looked back at her salad as she murmured, 'He loved the jigsaw puzzle.'

'I enjoyed doing it with him. Tammy, I know I was at fault on Saturday—'

'I think we both were. I'll let you have the death certificate for your aunt later.'

He shook his head. 'I don't think it's needed now. She

surprised me, actually. I've told her how alike Jake is, to James as a child, and she can't wait to meet him. Perhaps we could arrange something sooner rather than later.'

'I'll try and take him next weekend.'

'I'm on call then. Couldn't we go one evening?'

'I think the weekend will be best.' Convenient even, as she wanted to do it alone. 'Jake would be too tired in the evening.' She pushed back her chair and said, 'Duty calls. See you on the ward.'

CHAPTER SEVEN

BEN caught up with Tammy as she reached the ward entrance and grasped her arm to prevent her pushing open the door.

'Can we meet up after work?' His tone was urgent. 'I want to talk about us.'

'Us? Us?' she repeated incredulously. 'Ben, there is no *us*. I think we've both got far too much baggage from the past for that.'

Freeing herself, she crashed open the rubber doors and strode into the ward, where she settled to catch up on some paperwork at the centre table. But her thoughts weren't wholly on what she was doing.

A long afternoon stretched ahead. She would much have preferred to have kept her mind occupied with work, but it was typical that they weren't on take for emergencies and the patients they already had wanted peace to doze.

Even the outpatient clinic was not the usual mad rush. Mike had left at lunchtime to attend a conference, so no new patients were attending. Ben and Tammy coped easily with the follow-ups.

She was delighted to see Mr Wilbur there—and doing quite well, considering all the problems he had.

'You must be looked after well,' Tammy told him jokingly after checking his chest. 'That sounds much better.'

'I've got the best wife a man could have. I've always been her number one priority and she's never gone to work. I think that's where a lot of marriages fail these days.'

Tammy nodded, remembering what had been said about Deanna—probably just as well they'd found out before they'd married, although she was pretty sure Ben would find it hard to find a wife as submissive as Jack Wilbur had.

She was on her way back to the ward when her bleeper told her Jan needed her as there was a problem. 'Tammy, thank goodness. Stan Burt is sinking fast. Could you take a look at him and then have a word with his wife? I'm sure she'd rather hear the news from you than a stranger.'

Tammy checked Stan's condition herself before calling his wife into the office.

'He's dying, isn't he?'

Tammy nodded. 'I'm afraid so.'

She took Mrs Burt's hands as tears rolled down her face. 'I know it's for the best. He didn't want to suffer any more.'

'He's done much better than we expected, but it's got to the stage where he has no quality left in his life.'

She nodded. 'I know. I think I'd best get back to him now.'

'Would you like me to stay with you?'

'I'd like that.'

They made their way to his bedside only just in time. Five minutes later he drew his last breath. Mrs Burt indicated she would like to be alone with him, so Tammy returned to the office and found Ben there.

To her relief, he must have recognised her sombre mood and apart from asking 'Mr Burt?' he allowed her to sit quietly and annotate the time of death.

When she'd finished and had managed to collect her thoughts, he crossed the room to place a hand on her shoulder. 'Anything I can do?'

His empathy after their earlier exchange brought a lump to her throat. Perhaps he was still the understanding and caring doctor she had thought she knew. Even if his handling of personal relationships left a lot to be desired.

She shook her head. 'But I do need to tell Bob Grant and Harry Knut. They'd all become so close.'

He suggested they do it together. 'And then I think we could see about discharging those two. They are both so much better I think they'd be happier at home now.'

For the remainder of the afternoon Tammy occupied herself as best she could. She didn't see Ben again until she was unlocking her car and he came racing across the car park towards her.

'Tammy!' He was breathing deeply from the exertion.

She didn't speak but lifted her head to indicate she was listening.

'Look, I don't want to delay you now but, please, please, please, could we meet later?'

'Not possible unless I've arranged in advance for Lauren to stay home.'

He sighed. 'At the house, then? Once Jake is in bed?'

'Aren't you on call this evening?'

'George is covering for me until midnight.' He was leaning on the opposite side of the car as he spoke. 'Please, Tammy. It's important.'

'Who for? You? Me? Or your aunt?' She was tempted to jump into the car, slam the door and drive off, but she resisted the temptation. Allowing him to fall flat on his face was not the way to treat her boss, however she felt about him.

Torn as to what was the best course of action, she hesitated. She had to be sensible—they had to continue to work together and the patients must come first. She knew he was right but she wasn't prepared to make things easy for him and she wanted to think through a plan of campaign first.

'Maybe tomorrow. I'll tell Lauren I'll be later home.'

'You're not on call?'

'Wednesday.' She climbed into the car and started the engine.

He reluctantly moved away and raised a hand in farewell. She put the car in gear and, spinning the wheels, left the car park at speed.

Ben didn't move until her car was out of sight, then he sighed heavily and made his way back to the hospital. He knew he'd put himself into an impossible position as far as Tammy was concerned. His only excuse was that, despite recognising at an early age the flaws in his cousin's character, learning of his death had upset him more than he would have believed when he hadn't seen him for many years. The realisation that Jake was related to him as well had only really sunk in when his aunt had suggested they try to get custody of Jake.

'You've no grounds,' he'd told her gently.

'He's my grandson.'

'And Tammy is his mother.'

'But the boy is left to the ministrations of a nanny all day. That's not right. I can give him my undivided attention.'

It had taken a lot of argument for him to convince her that resorting to the law would be futile, though he had promised to persuade Tammy to allow the boy to meet his grandmother.

He groaned, berating himself for not leaving it to his aunt to ferret out the answers to her queries about James, instead of making himself the fall guy. He was too tied up emotionally with everyone concerned. Second thoughts told him that he couldn't have done that. He owed his aunt that much for all the years she'd been like a mother to him.

He walked back to his room in the residency and immediately regretted not having to work until midnight. Needing something to keep his mind occupied rather than gazing at four walls, he made his way down to the estate agent handling the house he was hoping to buy.

'What's happening about the surveyor's report?'

'It's being sorted as quickly as possible, Dr Davey.' The agent said the same thing every time he paid them a visit.

He decided to take another look at the house himself and made his way on foot to the nearby road.

As he approached he saw police tape blocking his way and frowned. Approaching the tape, he spoke to a constable. 'What's happened?'

'Car accident,' was the terse reply.

'I'm a doctor from the hospital. Does anyone need help?'

'All sorted,' the policeman told him. 'We're just taking measurements and then we'll open the road.'

'Can I walk through to number eighty-two?'

The policeman lifted the tape. 'I don't see why not. Nothing to see now.' Ben rounded the slight bend and gasped in horror at the mangled wreck of the two cars. He looked closer and to his dismay confirmed his fear that one of them was Tammy's Peugeot.

Remembering the reckless way she had driven out of the car park, he was momentarily overcome by a sinking feeling, then, still feeling nauseous, he collared one of the policemen holding a measuring tape. 'I'm from the hospital. A doctor. I'm pretty sure the blue car belongs to my colleague. Was she—anyone,' he corrected himself, 'injured?'

'Couldn't say, sir. I've only just taken over here. I gather some casualties have been taken to the hospital, though.'

The chap probably could say but, quite correctly, wasn't prepared to. Ben turned and raced back the way he had come.

He was breathless when he reached the accident and emergency department and, unable to speak, he searched the list of names on the whiteboard. Not finding Tammy's, he raced back to the reception desk. 'Hi, Jane. Is Dr Penrose here?'

'In the resus room. She—'

His heart in his mouth, he muttered, 'Thanks.' He didn't wait to hear more. Filled with trepidation, he raced along the corridor in search of Tammy, dreading what he was about to find. 'Please, God, let her be all right. Please, please, keep her safe,' he whispered. Her son needed her and so did he. He couldn't lose her now. He loved her.

He pushed open the door and tried to see what was happening. The face that beckoned him in belonged to Tammy. He felt his chin drop and stared at her in amazement. 'It's you. You're not...'

She frowned. 'Not what?'

'I—I imagined...' he stuttered as he tried to collect his thoughts. 'I... Thank God you're OK, Tam, love.' He inhaled deeply.

His relief at seeing her there as large as life made him want to take her in his arms and never let her go. But unfortunately the resuscitation room wasn't the place. 'I—I'll wait outside,' he told her. 'You'll need a lift home.'

She shrugged and turned her attention back to the patient on the trolley. He shuddered and prayed that he would find a way to allay her present hostility towards him.

It wasn't long before she joined him. 'I was supernumerary in there. I just stayed to see if they needed any help.'

'You weren't driving? I thought...' He let his voice tail off as a shudder rippled through his body at the thought of what he'd imagined.

She looked at him in amazement. 'Are you all right, Ben?'

'I saw your car. I thought...'

'You thought...?'

'You were involved in the accident.'

'I see! No. I was indoors. When I heard the smash I
rushed out and did what I could for the man at the scene
and on the way here. Even though I'm livid at what he's
done to my car.'

'Thank God you weren't in it.' Encircling her with his
arms, he hugged her as he'd wanted to when he'd found
her.

Trying to keep her distance by placing her hands on his
chest, she murmured, 'Hey, remember where we are.' Then
her lips curled into an impish smile. 'I get it now. You
thought I'd continued driving the way I left the car park,
didn't you? That in my temper I'd smashed into some poor
defenceless driver.'

'We-ell…'

Tammy shook her head. 'I've got a child, Ben. I can't
believe you think I would do something so irresponsible.'

'So what *were* you doing there?'

'As I got off duty on time for once, I paid my mother a
brief visit.'

Of course. He'd forgotten she'd said her parents lived in
that road.

'Do you want to ring Lauren? She must wonder where
you are.'

'No problem. Mum and Dad went straight over there. I
do have phone calls to make, though. I need to talk to the
insurers about a replacement car until mine can be fixed.'

'Tammy,' he said, gently taking hold of her arm, 'you
didn't take a close look at your car? I'm sorry to be the
one to tell you this but I imagine it's a write-off. He must
have hit it at speed.'

She stopped in her tracks and looked up at him. 'It can't
be. I—I…'

'Car insured through the medical association?'

She nodded.

'Should be no problem, then. We can ring them from my room. I have the number.'

Against her better judgement, Tammy allowed herself to be led into the residency and into a room that was crammed full of too many personal belongings.

'Sorry about the mess. I need to get into my own house. I was chasing up the sale this evening when I saw the accident.'

'I've delayed you.'

'Not really. The house is empty and I couldn't have got in. But I just had to get out of here into the fresh air.'

'I can imagine.' Her teeth worried guiltily at her bottom lip. It couldn't be very pleasant for Ben, living here. She could easily make a spare room if she moved Jake in with her, but there was no way that would be sensible.

'I hope you soon get something sorted.'

'I'm wondering if I wouldn't be better renting something after all.'

He couldn't have known what she was thinking. Could he? 'It wouldn't be the same.'

He unearthed the telephone and handed it to her. 'I have the insurer's number here somewhere.' He was already searching through his own papers.

'Don't bother. It's here in my bag.'

'Can I get you a coffee? Sorry I've nothing stronger.'

She shook her head. 'As soon as I've done this I must get back to Jake.'

She made the necessary phone calls, then told him, 'They can't do anything about a replacement car until tomorrow, so would you mind if I rang Dad? He'll come and collect me.'

He gently removed the receiver from her hand. 'No need for that. I'll take you home.'

'Thanks.' She had not had a chance to tell her parents about Ben being Jazz's cousin so the last thing she wanted was to feel obliged to ask him in to meet them. She had hoped to deflect him from offering her a lift, but she knew she shouldn't have expected anything else.

They walked out to his car in silence, and as he ushered her into the passenger seat he said, 'Try not to worry. I'll arrange with George that I leave early and come and collect you in time for work in the morning.'

'There's no need.'

'There's every need and I'd like to do it.'

She nodded her acceptance. 'Thanks, then.'

When he pulled up outside her house, she tentatively invited him in. 'Although Jake will be in bed by now, I guess.'

Sensing her reluctance, he uttered a resigned sigh. 'Perhaps another night. Half-seven all right in the morning?'

Her mother and father were drinking tea in the kitchen. 'Jake's already in bed. He's fine. How did you get home?'

Tammy had expected it to be the first question her mother asked, and she had planned her response.

'My registrar brought me.'

She watched a knowing look pass between her mother and father. 'That's nice. Is he the doctor who brought Jake the puzzle on Saturday?'

So Jake had been talking. 'It was, but it's not what you think, Mum.'

'You don't know what I'm thinking.'

'Oh, yes, I do. Is he single and an all-round good man?' Tammy laughed. 'Actually, the reason he came to the house on Saturday was because he wanted to see Jake, not me.'

'Jake?' Her mother frowned.

She took a deep breath. 'He's discovered that Jazz is—was his cousin.'

Her mother's mouth dropped open. 'His cousin?'

Tammy knew if she'd said he was an alien her parents wouldn't have been any more surprised.

'But—but—Jazz always said he had no one.'

'I'm beginning to think there's a lot we didn't know about him. His real name is—was James. James Walton.'

'How did you find out?'

'I'll tell you. But not yet. When we're eating.'

'You look done in. How about a take-away? You choose.'

As they ate a little later, she told her parents the whole story. When she'd finished, her mother remained thoughtful.

'So what are you going to do?'

'Make contact with Jake's grandmother, I suppose. It's only right now that I know about her.'

Her mother nodded. 'I bet she won't believe it until she sets her eyes on him. I know I wouldn't. It's like something from a book.'

'Mum,' Tammy began slowly, 'if she wants to meet him, would you and Dad be willing to take him for me?'

'Of course we would, love, but why?'

Tammy sighed deeply. 'I'm not sure that I want to get any more involved with the family than I already am.'

'You mean…?'

'I don't know what I mean at the moment, Mum. I just need to know you'd do it for me if I can't face it.'

'We'll do it. No fear. Now, you stop worrying about something that might never happen. You've got enough to think about with your car.'

Tammy smiled gratefully at her father. She could usually count on him to intervene when her mother started to ask too many questions.

Her parents left soon after that and with a sigh of relief Tammy settled back in the deep armchair to think.

Introducing Jake to his grandmother was probably the only thing she was certain was right. Ben was more of a problem.

She thought about his obvious concern about her when he'd thought she'd been injured in the accident. And even when he'd found out that she hadn't been, he must have realised she was shaken by the incident and he hadn't been able to do enough for her.

Nothing added up. Ben's inconsistencies and the unspoken messages he'd been giving out since the day they'd met left her increasingly bewildered and she didn't know what to make of him. He seemed to have unfathomable depths and yet he was certainly one of the most considerate and caring men she had ever met. One thing was for sure. It was a pretty unusual situation to find themselves in and she couldn't blame him if he was as confused as she was.

She decided to sleep on it. She'd missed seeing Jake tonight and she intended to be up early to spend some time with him before she went to work.

Her internal alarm clock woke her at six as planned, but Jake's wasn't so co-operative. She'd enjoyed a leisurely breakfast and was waiting for Ben to arrive when she heard Jake jump out of bed.

She raced upstairs and gathered him into a hug. 'Sorry I didn't get home last night before you went to bed.'

He chuckled, obviously delighted to see her. 'You *will* be home tonight, though, won't you?'

'I hope so, Jake. My car's broken and I'm waiting for another one, but I should have something to drive by then.'

'Grandma said a stupid man hit it with his car.'

The doorbell rang and Lauren trailed out of her bedroom and down the stairs to answer it.

'It's a Dr Davey,' she called up to Tammy.

'I'm just coming.'

Jake was ahead of her, tumbling down the last couple of stairs in his eagerness to see his new friend. 'Are you coming to play with me, Ben?'

Tammy's heart ached as she watched him tenderly ruffle

Jake's hair. 'I'm afraid not. I have to take your mummy to the hospital. She has to work today. We both do.'

The boy nodded solemnly. 'When will you come, then?'

Tammy was embarrassed. 'Don't pester him, Jake.'

He stuck his bottom lip out in a pout. 'He helped me with my puzzle.'

'And I will do again, I promise. When it's not a working day.'

Despite her misgivings, Ben's reply sent a shaft of warmth scudding through Tammy.

'We have to go now.' Tammy kissed her son. 'See you tonight. Be a good boy.'

He looked at Ben and offered him his hand. 'Boys don't kiss each other, do they?'

Ben took the tiny hand in his and said, 'No, we shake hands. See you soon, Jake.'

They made their way to Ben's car with Lauren and Jake watching and waving from the window.

'Jake won't forget that promise.'

Ben didn't speak until they were settled in his car. 'I don't make a habit of letting people down. I'd like to see Jake again, Tammy. And sooner rather than later. But when or, I suppose if depends on you.' As if trying to gauge her reaction, he glanced at her briefly before returning his eyes to the road.

'I'm sure you have plenty to fill what little spare time you have without that but if you want to see him, you're welcome any time. Jake thinks you're great.'

He glanced at her again. 'Nice to know that somebody does.'

Tammy felt a flush beginning to spread across her cheeks. 'Fishing for compliments?'

They were queuing to get into the car park and he took one hand off the wheel and rested it lightly on her thigh.

'This isn't easy, Tammy. For any of us. Like I said yester-day, we do need to talk. Big time.'

Conscious of the sensations just his touch was still ca-pable of arousing within her, she sighed then nodded. 'Per-haps once I've got the car sorted we can arrange it.'

He nodded. 'Not tonight? You're on call tomorrow and I am on Thursday and at the weekend.'

She shook her head. 'Probably not. I need to spend time with Jake.'

'But later. We could eat. And talk.'

Tammy was hesitant. She guessed it would be sensible to clear the air between them, but her emotions were shot to pieces after the events of the past few days and she wasn't sure she could handle any meeting with him ration-ally until she had them more under control. 'I'll ring Lauren and see if she'll be around tonight.'

'I'd appreciate that.'

Hopefully the insurance company would have organised some replacement transport for her by that time.

Ben followed her onto the ward, his thoughts churning fu-riously. Her vivacity was what had first attracted him to her and since Saturday it had almost disappeared. She looked as if she had the cares of the world on her shoulders and he knew many of them were his fault.

Sure Deanna had caused him pain in the past but that was no reason not to trust Tammy. Warm, loving, kind Tammy, the best doctor he'd had to assist him since the hospital had opened, and the most affectionate one, he thought with a wry grimace.

Jan welcomed them on duty with open arms. 'Thank goodness you're both here. All hell's been let loose. Three new patients on their way up and only two beds.'

'Do you know what their problems are?'

'A tension pneumothorax following a fight, one of our

longstanding coal miners and an asthmatic patient who has succumbed to this perishing infection and is not responding to antibiotics.'

Ben grimaced. 'The asthmatic and the chap with the collapsed lung will have to come here. I'll take a quick look at the miner and see if he can be boarded out.'

'While you're gone I'll take a look at what's been happening here overnight. I'll try again to get a bed in the geriatric unit for Billy Old. If not, we'll have to transfer him to a sleeper bed.'

Tammy picked up the overnight report as Jan told her, 'Before you get immersed in that, could you take a quick look at Mr Dennis, Tammy? He seems to be deteriorating again.'

She nodded and followed Jan into the ward. Mr Dennis was propped on a mound of pillows, gasping for breath despite the oxygen being delivered to him from the piped supply.

Tammy gave him a reassuring smile and took out her stethoscope. As she checked his pulse, she asked Jan, 'How long's he been like this?'

The patient made an attempt to say something that resulted in a spluttering cough. She rested a hand over his. 'Don't try and talk until you feel better.'

Jan checked the records. 'About an hour.'

'And he's had his nebuliser?'

She checked again and nodded. 'At six.'

Tammy gently opened his pyjamas and carefully listened to his chest. 'Take as deep a breath as you can, Mr Dennis.'

'It seems to be settling, but I think I need to check with Dr Davey about increasing the dosage of some of your drugs.'

Jan had been right. It *was* like all hell let loose and it continued that way throughout the day, with pressure on beds adding to the problems of the many really sick patients. The one good thing was when she found a bed where Billy could be cared for without having to move him again in the future. By the time she realised that there had been no word from the insurers, it was far too late to do anything about it.

A few moments later Ben came in search of her. 'It's no problem, Tammy. I'll take you home and collect you again in the morning.'

It might be no problem to him but it was to her. 'I can get a taxi.'

'There's no need. It's quietening down a bit here at the moment.'

This time he accepted the invitation to come in. Lauren was in the living room, reading to a pyjama-clad Jake, who immediately left Lauren and flung himself first at Tammy then at Ben.

'Sorry, Tammy.' Lauren was studying Ben with interest. 'He's had his bath but he wanted to wait up and see you.'

Jake tugged at Ben's jacket. 'You read me a story.'

'Please,' Tammy corrected automatically. 'Thanks, Lauren. I'm sorry to be so late. Hope I haven't delayed you.'

'I'm not meeting Marcus till eight.' She handed the book to Ben and settled in the other armchair to listen.

Not having mentioned his previous visits to Lauren, Tammy was uneasy. 'If you're in a hurry, Ben, I can do it.'

'No problem,' he assured her. 'Perhaps we can talk afterwards.'

Lauren bounced up from her chair. 'Can I get you both something to eat or drink before I go?'

Realising the impossible position she was in, Tammy turned to Ben with a querying lift of her eyebrows.

'That would be great, if you don't mind.'

'No problem at all,' Lauren trilled, making her way through to the kitchen.

'Shall we get you into bed before Ben reads the story?' Tammy asked Jake.

After a moment, he nodded. 'Like Saturday?'

'That's right. I'll come up and tuck you in and Ben can read to you. Say goodnight to Lauren.'

Excitedly Jake did as he was told and allowed Tammy to give him a big hug before taking herself back downstairs. 'Sorry about this, Lauren. What can I do to help?'

'A salad. I'd made a pasta dish and it just needed popping into the oven.'

'I can manage now if you want to get away.'

Lauren checked her watch. 'I don't need to go yet.'

Tammy heard Ben coming back down the stairs and sighed. Her original intention had been to talk to Ben over their drinks, but the nanny's presence now made that impossible. She poured three glasses of wine.

Lauren was reluctant to leave and hung on Ben's every word, frustrating Tammy's need to clear the air between them as she had realised, with the distance of time, that she had rather overreacted the previous Saturday. Eventually, she looked at her watch and said to Lauren, 'Aren't you meeting Marcus at eight?'

'Goodness, I didn't realise.' Lauren shot out of the front door at speed.

Having poured another glass of wine for them both, Tammy told Ben, 'I'll just go and check on supper.'

He followed her into the kitchen a few moments later. 'Anything I can do to help?'

She handed him cutlery. 'You could set the table.'

'Can't we eat in here?'

She shrugged. 'Not very salubrious.'

'But cosy. And hopefully we won't be interrupted. I thought Lauren was never going to leave.'

'I thought you were enjoying chatting with her.'

'She seems nice, but she made me feel old!'

Tammy laughed. 'I know what you mean.'

'You're not much older than she is.'

'Maybe not in years, but I'm a mother.'

'So?'

'I aged overnight when Jake was born. I suppose it's the responsibility. And being a doctor makes it worse.'

Ben laughed. 'I can think of a few who are still as immature as they were as first-year students! Peter, for instance!'

'He needs to be taken in hand by a good woman...' She'd realised what she'd said had been a mistake the moment she'd started, and she didn't know how to finish.

'Do you think that applies to me as well?'

Colour flooded into her cheeks and she shook her head. 'You don't behave the way Peter does.'

'In other words, I'm old and boring?'

Tammy turned sharply to deny that wasn't what she'd meant at all, then saw by the glint in his eye that he was winding her up.

'You know perfectly well that's not what I meant.' She threw the oven glove she was holding at him and turned back to her cooking.

Ben caught it and in one stride crossed the kitchen. Catching her in his arms, he spun her to face him. 'That's more like the Tammy I thought I knew. It's wonderful to see you relaxing.'

She raised both hands and pushed him away. 'No, Ben. I'm exhausted and, like you said, we need to talk. And eat. That's what I invited you in for. Nothing else.'

He nodded. 'OK, but only after I've apologised again for Saturday. I didn't handle a difficult situation as I should have...'

She shrugged. 'I can understand how upset you must have been.'

'We were both upset, but that was no excuse—'

'Forget it. I have.'

He released her reluctantly.

She served out two plates of pasta and offered him the salad bowl.

When they'd both finished eating, she said, 'I'd be grateful if you could tell me where Jazz…er…James's mother lives. I thought if I contact her soon, she will be more used to the idea when the time came.'

His voice was now quiet and serious. 'If you haven't got your car sorted, I'll take you. I'll find someone to cover for me.'

'No! This is something I want—need—to do on my own.'

'The house is isolated and difficult to find. Impossible to reach by public transport, unless you go on a Wednesday. And then it's only one bus each way morning and lunchtime.'

'I should have a car by then. Even if I have to pay for its hire myself.'

'The house is still not easy to find.'

'I'll manage.'

'Are you independent or what?'

'I've had to be.' Tammy watched as he wrote his aunt's name and address and the telephone number.

'I'll try and ring her later.'

'It's not going to be easy for either of you. She's not very well disposed to you at the moment.'

'I know. I'll tread carefully, I promise.'

Ben nodded. 'If you let me know when it's arranged, I'll try and have a chat with her first. The more she talks about it, the better. She even started saying she'd try to get custody of him, which I told her was ridiculous, but she thinks you neglect him by going out to work.'

Things began to slide into place. Like the change in his manner towards her after a visit to his aunt. 'It was probably grief talking.'

He gave a wicked grin and said, 'She said your name was some "fancy foreign frippery"!'

'You made that up.'

'Nothing to do with me. It was her words exactly. I like the name—prefer Tam to Tammy, I have to say—but I like Tamsin best of all.'

'Hmm.'

'Anyway, what I'm trying to say is that I'm not sure how she will react to you.'

There was a sudden scream from upstairs and a startled Tammy rushed to see what was the matter, followed closely by Ben.

CHAPTER EIGHT

JAKE was clutching his stomach and still screaming, so Tammy lifted him onto her knee and tried to calm him.

The next minute he was violently sick. She looked up at Ben, who was hovering at the door to see what the problem was. 'I think you'd better go, Ben. There's a bug doing the rounds at his nursery group and he's obviously picked it up.'

She rocked Jake over her shoulder and said, 'It seems to be pretty virulent. The last thing we need is for both of us to be off with it.'

He nodded. 'If you're sure that's all it is and there's nothing I can do to help?'

Cuddling the now quiet child to her, she shook her head. 'I need to clean us both up and then try to settle him.' She smiled. 'But many thanks for the lift tonight.'

'Unless you ring, I'll be along at the same time in the morning.'

'You don't have to. I can always get a taxi.'

'Maybe, but there's no need because I'll be here,' he told her firmly, and left.

Lauren did not arrive home until the early hours of the morning, so Tammy slept only fitfully between repeated checks on Jake. This meant her mind worked overtime on the problem of how the meeting with Jazz's mother was likely to go.

Until Ben's comments the previous evening, she had stupidly imagined Mrs Walton would be so delighted to have this tangible reminder of her dead son that they would be welcomed with open arms. Now she wasn't so sure. She knew Ben was right, that the woman would have no legal claim to Jake, but she could make things very unpleasant indeed for Tammy.

Despite the initial shock when Ben had recognised his cousin's photograph, she'd gradually accepted that Jazz had had relatives she'd never known existed and who would be an extended family for Jake. But if they weren't happy about the situation, she didn't intend to subject her son to any hostility and would refuse to allow them access.

Jake looked pale the next morning but seemed better. 'Don't take him to nursery school today, Lauren. I'll be in touch. I could do without being on call tonight. I'll see if I can get someone to stand in for me for a short time so that I can pop home and see him. Although he's probably over the worst already.'

Lauren shrugged. 'I'll ring you if there's a problem.'

'Thanks, Lauren. Did you have a good time last night?'

'Not really. I split with Marcus.'

'I'm sorry.'

'Don't be. He was so immature. Not like that doctor last night. Now, he was really something. Is he your—?'

'No, Lauren. He's not my anything. We work together and he's been giving me lifts because the insurers haven't replaced my car as yet. That's all.'

'Lovely butt.'

Seeing Ben's car pull alongside the kerb saved Tammy from having to answer. 'That's him now. I don't want to keep him waiting. I'll ring later.'

She sped out to the car, only too aware of Lauren waving and smiling in Ben's direction.

He raised a hand in acknowledgement and opened the passenger door for Tammy.

'How's Jake?'

'A bit under the weather but he hasn't been sick again

and has only a slight temperature. He's very clingy, though.'

'I'm not surprised. Is he drinking?'

'Only a sip so far, but Lauren will let me know if there's a problem.'

'What about your on-call duty tonight?'

'He'll probably be fine by then. You know as well as I do how quickly children bounce back.'

'If there's a problem...'

'I'm sure there won't be.'

'If there is, I can stand in for you,' he persisted.

'Thanks, Ben. I might take you up on that for half an hour or so, but I'll see what Lauren says about him later.'

'You'll take that hare-brained nanny of yours' word for it?'

Tammy smiled, secretly pleased at his description of Lauren. 'She's looked after Jake for a couple of years now. She's not as flighty as she appears. Believe me. I wouldn't leave him with someone I didn't trust.'

To her relief it was a much quieter day on the ward. Late in the afternoon she was working with Ben on stabilising Mr Dennis's condition again when an insurance representative came to talk to her about her car.

When he wanted Tammy to go with him to discuss a replacement, Ben told her to go and take as long as she needed.

It was well over an hour before she returned. She rushed into the ward office where Ben was talking to Jan. 'Sorry about that.'

He swung round and with a serious face said accusingly, 'Your mobile phone wasn't switched on.'

What on earth had she done, or left undone, that he'd needed to contact her so urgently? 'I left it in my coat pocket.' She slipped her white coat on and held it out for him to see. 'I'm really sorry for that, Ben, and for having taken so long. At least I have wheels now and won't trouble you any more.'

'Tammy, that doesn't matter!'

She was suddenly aware of his grave expression.

'Lauren rang. She was worried about Jake. When I couldn't contact you I told her to bring him to A and E.'

'What?'

'Jake's down there now, waiting for a second opinion.'

'Meningitis,' Tammy whispered, voicing the fears of every parent. 'I should have been there. I must go to him.'

Ben caught her arm. 'It's not meningitis, Tammy, but it just could be his appendix.'

Determined not to be kept from her son any longer, Tammy shrugged her arm free. Ben walked with her. 'Calm down, Tammy. Lauren was very sensible. Because we know there's a bug doing the rounds, it's easy to assume that a child who is sick has caught it, but it is better to be safe than sorry.'

'If that's a criticism, perhaps you could leave it until I know what's happening to Jake.' She stalked off at speed.

The paediatrician was leaving the department as they arrived and Ben hailed him. 'David, this is Jake's mother.'

He gave Tammy a reassuring smile. 'I don't think it's anything more to worry about than a tummy bug but if so it's a nasty one. Keep a close eye on him and call me if you're worried.'

Lauren appeared from behind a cubicle curtain at that moment. 'I'm so sorry, Tammy, to have caused all this fuss, but I was so frightened for Jake. He is so hot.'

Tammy nodded and went though to her son. 'Hello, Jake.' She sat down beside him and smoothed his forehead.

He opened one eye and murmured, 'Can I stay here with you, Mummy?'

'I think it'll be best if you take him home and stay there.'

Ben had followed her behind the curtains. 'I'll rearrange the on-call rota. If no one else can do it, I'll take tonight's.'

'I—I can't, Ben.' She whispered.

'You can't what?' He looked almost fierce.

'Let everyone down.'

He uttered a deep sigh. 'If you're talking about the ward, you can and you will. Jake's the one who's important now. You are not letting him down.' Although his voice was quiet, he spoke the words emphatically.

She felt suddenly defensive of her parenting skills. 'Lauren is always there.'

'But you're not.'

'What are you trying to say?' Her tone was glacial.

'Tammy, Jake needs you tonight. I'd say the same to any parent in this situation, male or female, single or married.'

She nodded. He was right, of course. If the ward was covered for her shift, she was letting no one down but Jake. Trying to prove she was a superwoman didn't matter. Jake did.

'If you're sure?'

Ben nodded. 'Very sure, and I promise no one will accuse you of dereliction of duty!'

She smiled. 'Thanks, Ben. I owe you. Thank goodness I've got a car outside. You wait here with Jake, Lauren.'

She made her way to the car park cocooned in a warmth created by the knowledge that somebody cared enough to do her on-call duty for her son's sake. She felt even happier that that person was Ben and actually smiled as she climbed into her replacement Peugeot—silver this time.

Jake's illness meant no visit to Mrs Walton that weekend. Tammy decided to try again for the following one, and as he was off duty, Ben said he would take her. Having learnt how Mrs Walton had reacted to the news that she had a grandson, Tammy felt she definitely needed to meet her first before allowing Jake to visit. There were too many details she didn't want her son to overhear, especially as any hostility towards Tammy would upset him and threaten any future relationship between the boy and his grand-mother.

And that would be sad. For the same reason she agreed to go with Ben.

As she had predicted, Jake soon bounced back to health and by that time he was eating and drinking normally, so Tammy could see no reason not to leave him with her parents on Saturday afternoon.

She explained to her mother how she felt. 'So would you mind looking after Jake for a couple of hours?'

'No problem. You know we enjoy it.'

Ben collected her at three, by which time Tammy was feeling somewhat apprehensive.

'Please, don't take anything she says personally,' Ben pleaded after greeting her with a kiss. 'James was her only son and her life has been consumed by her search for him. She's not finding it easy and she needs someone to blame.'

Tammy nodded. 'Give me credit for some understanding, Ben.'

He groaned and pulled her close. 'I'm sorry, Tam, but I'm worried. She is so convinced that his leaving home, and now his death, is your fault. It could result in a very unpleasant couple of hours for you.'

'That's one of the reasons I've decided to leave Jake with Mum and Dad. I'm prepared for her initial bitterness, but I hope she'll soon accept that I have nothing to reproach myself for, Ben.'

'I just hope that nothing is said that will harm the future for any of us. You and Jake mean far too much to me now and I know that in time, if only she'll allow it, you could to her.'

As he set the car in motion Tammy forgot her fears as

she savoured his words. 'You and Jake mean far too much to me now.'

When Ben had introduced her to the serious-faced lady who was unmistakably a relative of both Jazz and Ben, Tammy smiled and said, 'Good afternoon, Mrs Walton. I'm so pleased to meet you at last.'

'Yes. Yes.' She stared at Tammy as if unable to believe this could possibly be the woman she had searched for so long.

Tammy handed her the flowers she had brought.

'That's kind of you.' The older woman looked at the gift with distaste, as if she thought it anything but. 'Go through to the conservatory and I'll put these in water and get some refreshment.' She indicated the open patio doors leading from the dining room.

Ben took Tammy through and they stood silently looking at the garden. Tammy took a couple of deep breaths of the fresh air to steady her resolve and Ben slipped his arm around her shoulders and squeezed reassuringly.

When their hostess reappeared, Tammy made an effort to lighten the mood. 'Your garden is lovely. Bringing you those flowers was like taking coals to Newcastle.'

'Yes. It was.' After placing a tray of tea on the conservatory table, she continued to stare at Tammy with something akin to hatred in her eyes. 'Why did you take my James away from me?'

Ben was about to speak in Tammy's defence but Tammy stopped him. 'Mrs Walton,' she said quietly, 'I did not take your son away. Jazz, as he called himself then, told me he had no relatives whatsoever. Believe me, it caused problems enough when he was killed and I knew nothing about him. The police wanted a birth certificate and I'm sorry to say I could find nothing relating to his early days. He had certainly covered his tracks well.'

'You weren't married, I hear.'

Compressing her lips, Tammy shook her head.

'So your son is illegitimate.'

The bald statement hurt Tammy nearly as much as Jazz's rejection of her pregnancy. She clenched her fists to prevent herself from saying something she would regret and felt Ben rest a restraining hand on her arm.

'I don't think there's any call for that kind of talk, is there?' He was clearly furious.

'Jake wasn't born until after the accident,' Tammy said, glacially.

Tears poured down the older lady's face at the mention of her son's death and Ben moved to comfort her, but she pulled away from his touch.

The verbal harangue started again and the forgotten tea went cold. Tammy was subjected to a barrage of questions about their life together and Jazz's death and the funeral, but there was no further mention of Jake.

Ben intervened on several occasions, but his aunt ignored him.

By the end of an hour Tammy could take no more. She felt as if she had been physically battered and needed to escape. Nothing she could say seemed to make any impression on Jazz's mother and she decided the visit had been a mistake. She turned to Ben. 'I think it would be best if I leave now.'

Mrs Walton, who had been watching her hands as she tore a damp tissue into little pieces, jerked her head up and snapped, 'When can I see my grandson?'

After all that had been said Tammy hadn't expected that and she wasn't sure it would be a sensible move unless some of the issues were resolved between his mother and grandmother first.

'I'm prepared to bring him when it's convenient, but—'

'You'll bring him tomorrow?'

Tammy hesitated and looked at Ben. That wasn't what

she had intended, and she didn't want Jake upset by the kind of treatment she'd received.

'Please, Miss Penrose?'

'I'd like you to call me Tammy.'

'Ben tells me Jake looks like James at a similar age.'

Annoyed that the older woman had ignored her offer, Tammy sighed. 'As far as I can see from the photographs, yes.'

'So you'll bring him to see me tomorrow, Tammy?'

'That's OK by me,' Ben said quietly. 'I can bring him.'

Tammy knew that, however she felt, for Jake's sake she had to be the one who came with him whenever she arranged it. 'I'll try for tomorrow afternoon.'

For the first time Mrs Walton managed a half-smile. 'I can't wait.'

Tammy hesitated and then said, 'I'd rather we didn't talk about the accident in front of Jake. He knows his father died and I think that's enough at his age.'

'He's four, isn't he?'

'Just. He should start school in September.'

'Thank you for coming, Tammy. Until tomorrow.' She hesitantly offered her hand.

Tammy took it, then impulsively leaned forward and kissed the older lady's cheek. 'We'll be here about three.'

Mrs Walton flushed, but this time didn't move away. 'Does Jake—I like that name—like chocolate cake?'

Tammy smiled at the small peace offering. 'Anything with chocolate.'

'Just like his dad.' Tears sprang to her eyes again and Tammy thought it was probably best to leave her to her memories.

'This is my telephone number,' Tammy said softly. 'If you want to ask me anything more, I'll be home all evening.'

'I do want to… Who will you say I am?'

Tammy started with surprise. 'His grandmother.'

She nodded. 'That's all right, then.'

Once they were back in Ben's car, Tammy said to him, 'That was a sudden thaw. I hope I'm doing the right thing. I don't want Jake upset by a reception like I received today or by her smothering him because he looks like her lost son.'

'I'll have a word with her this evening, Tammy. What are you doing later?'

'Nothing much, apart from when Mum brings Jake back from the shops.'

'Can I wait and see him?'

'Good idea. You can meet my mum.' But when Mrs Penrose dropped Jake off, she was in too much of a rush to do more than kiss Jake and Tammy and dash off.

'Why do I have to put this silly shirt on? Where are we going?' Jake asked as Tammy struggled to make him look presentable the next afternoon.

'To visit someone you've never met before.'

'Why?'

It was a difficult question to answer. 'Because Dr Davey asked me to.'

'Will Ben be there?'

'Yes—he's taking us.'

'Where does she live?'

'Way out in the country. Now, brush your hair and put your shoes on.'

Jake was eventually ready and then said petulantly, 'I'm thirsty.'

She rummaged in her bag and handed him a bottle of water and a tape of children's songs which, if necessary, would keep him occupied for most of the journey.

'Ben's here,' she told Jake a few moments later.

'What will this lady be like?'

'A bit like Grandma.'

He digested that information in silence before asking, as Tammy climbed into the front passenger seat and Ben welcomed her with a peck on her cheek, 'What shall I call her?'

'I think she'd like you to call her ''Grandma'', but for the moment ''Mrs Walton'' would be best.'

'Mrs Walton,' he repeated, 'Mrs Walton, the wally.'

'No! Just Mrs Walton, please.' Tammy caught Ben's eye and tried hard not to laugh. He was at the stage of making up silly names for everyone.

Mrs Walton must have been watching and opened the door even before Tammy could release Jake from his car seat.

She locked the car and took his hand. 'This is Jake.' He hung back behind her so she rested an arm round his shoulder to reassure him.

'Yes. Yes. I can see...' Mrs Walton's eyes were fixed on the boy. 'He's just like James as a boy.' Tears started to flow down her cheeks so Tammy quickly steered Jake through to the conservatory and Ben went with him.

'What will, er, Jake drink?' Mrs Walton called from the dining room, pausing in mopping her eyes to fix her gaze on the boy again as if she couldn't quite believe what she was seeing.

'Squash. Or water, please.'

When, a few minutes later, she handed Jake the glass from a tray containing cups of tea, he took it without a word.

'What do you say?' Tammy prompted.

'Thank you, Mrs Walton.'

'Call me, er, Grandma.'

'I already have a Grandma, thank you,' he answered.

'Most people have two, Jake,' Tammy told him gently. 'She could be your second.'

He gave them both a baleful look and buried his nose in the glass.

'Perhaps it's too soon.'

'Probably.'

'Does he know who I am?'

Tammy gave an imperceptible shake of her head. 'Not exactly.'

'Perhaps you and I can talk some more. Ben can look after Jake.'

'Ben's my friend,' Jake told her.

Tammy wasn't sure she could cope with Mrs Walton's organising. She was beginning to see why Jazz might have found it stifling.

Jake asked Tammy if he could go out into the garden.

She looked towards Mrs Walton for an answer.

'Of course. You can run around on the lawn. Keep out of the way of the gardener, though.'

He frowned. 'Gar-den-er?' he repeated.

Mrs Walton explained to Tammy. 'A man helps me to keep the garden nice. He comes most weekends. He's digging over some of the flower-beds today.'

'As long as you keep on the lawn, Jake, you'll be OK. Stay where we can see you.'

He nodded and ran out, leaving Tammy and her hostess to finish their tea. He came back almost immediately, his index finger to his lips.

Tammy frowned. 'What's the matter, Jake?'

'The gar-den-er's asleep. I might wake him.'

'Asleep?' Frowning, Mrs Walton leapt out of her chair and shot through the patio doors.

Curious, Ben and Tammy followed just as Mrs Walton shouted, 'He's dead, he's dead. Do something. Quickly.'

Grabbing her bag containing her mobile phone, Tammy followed Ben across the lawn, thinking there wasn't much they could do if he was dead.

When she reached the gardener, lying on the edge of the lawn by his spade, Ben was kneeling down beside him and had discovered a faint, rapid pulse. She took out her mobile phone and dialled 999 then, after asking for a resuscitation ambulance immediately, handed it to Mrs Walton to give them directions to the house.

The gardener's eyelids flickered and Tammy asked, 'What's his name?'

'Philip Burton.'

'Can you hear me, Philip?' Tammy asked in a loud voice.

He opened his eyelids a little further and gave a slight nod.

'Can you tell me what happened?'

He moved his tight hand across his chest and muttered, 'Pain.'

Tammy nodded and said quietly, 'Do you have angina?'

He appeared puzzled.

'Don't worry about it now. There's an ambulance on the way.'

'I think it's probably a heart attack.' Ben said quietly to Mrs Walton. 'Can you find me some cushions and perhaps a small blanket to make him comfortable? And do you have any aspirin?'

Mrs Walton hurried away and Tammy saw Jake hunkered against the wall, watching everything they were doing.

'It's all right Jake. We're going to help him to sit up. You can play on the other side of the lawn.'

He moved across, but Tammy saw he kept an eye on everything Ben was doing. She just hoped Philip wouldn't lapse into unconsciousness or, worse still, stop breathing.

She heard footsteps and looked up to see Mrs Walton laden with blankets and cushions. 'We can make you a bit more comfortable now,' she reassured Philip.

'No aspirin, I'm afraid. Only paracetamol.' Mrs Walton told her.

'Don't worry. I think I can hear the ambulance.' Tammy crouched down and placed two of the cushions to raise the gardener into a semi-sitting position and folded a blanket under his bent knees to prevent him slipping down.

''S better,' he murmured, as Ben's aunt went to open the front door to admit the paramedics.

Once he was loaded into the vehicle and being connected up to the various monitors, Tammy went to check that Jake was not too upset by what had happened.

Mrs Walton joined them. 'The ambulancemen would like Ben to go with them, Tammy. It's quite a long journey to the hospital and when I told them you're both doctors... Ben said you can drive his car and so I said if he rang, you would collect him.'

'That's OK. I can take Jake with me.'

'He can stay with me. You'd like that, wouldn't you, Jake? I've made you a chocolate cake.'

He nodded his head politely but Tammy could see he wasn't any keener than she was.

'He's quite a handful...'

'We'll be fine.'

Tammy was torn, but if Jake wasn't upset when the time came for her to leave, it would hurt Mrs Walton's feelings if she insisted she take him. There was nothing she could do but agree.

When Ben's call came, Jake's grandmother said, 'You'll be all right with me until Mum gets back with Ben, won't you?'

Jake didn't answer but looked appealingly at Tammy, which made her even more reluctant to leave him.

'Be a good boy, Jake. I'll be back as soon as I can.' She bent and kissed him and hurried out to the car.

When she got to the hospital Ben was waiting and she

pushed open the passenger door, eager to be away from Jake for as short a time as possible.

He leaned over to kiss her, but she was already moving the lever through the gears as she set off down the hospital perimeter road.

'What's the hurry?'

'I want to leave Jake for as short a time as possible.'

'You should have brought him.'

'Your aunt wanted him to stay. I—I couldn't refuse—she would have been so hurt.'

'He'll be OK—she's had children herself.'

He turned to look at her and laid a calming hand on her thigh. 'Hey, you're shaking. Don't get so uptight.'

'He hardly knows her.'

'You can't have been away that long. What do you think is going to happen?

'I—I don't really know.'

He sighed. 'I'll call my aunt to say we're on our way. Then we'll know if there's a problem.' He dialled the number.

She nodded. 'How is Philip?'

'Stable—and in good hands. That's about all I can say at the moment.' She could hear the telephone ringing and breathed a sigh of relief when it was answered. 'Hello. It's Ben. We're on our way back. All well?'

He listened for a couple of minutes and then terminated the call.

'What did she say?'

'Apparently Jake's thoroughly enjoying himself consuming a huge slice of chocolate cake.'

Tammy let out the breath she hadn't known she'd been holding. 'Thanks for that.'

'Can we slow down now?' he teased, then, seeing the tears of relief in her eyes, he said gently, 'Pull into that lay-by ahead and I'll take over.'

She nodded and did as he asked. 'Sorry about that. I know I'm silly...'

They exchanged seats and he frowned. 'Look, could we steal a little time for ourselves? I suggest Ye Olde Teashop in Platten.'

'I'm sorry, Ben, I'd rather get back. Jake...' She stopped, suddenly aware that he'd moved his hands to the sides of her cheeks and his head was bending towards hers. Powerless to prevent him kissing her, she moaned softly when their lips met. His mouth moved on hers, teasing and coaxing, until she was lost in a swirling mist of oblivion.

When he eventually relaxed his hold, she pulled abruptly away.

'You've got yourself into a right old state, haven't you?'

'Jake—'

'Will certainly be upset if he sees you like this.'

Tammy looked up to meet Ben's compassionate eyes looking down at her and, as if mesmerised, watched him lean towards her again and murmur, 'I think we have some unfinished business.'

A seismic tremor roared through her, its aftershock turning her legs to jelly. Acknowledging her need, he tightened his hold to tempt her to surrender to his demands. And she might have done had it not been for Jake.

'I sense your son is coming between us.' He sighed. 'I hoped you were beginning to realise how much you *both* mean to me.'

She looked up at him. 'You've been very good to Jake. We've a lot to thank you for...'

'But? I can hear the reservation in your voice.'

She bit at her lip, aware he was asking the impossible. If circumstances had been different perhaps, but she knew now that she loved him too much to allow him to alienate himself from his aunt, who meant so much to him. And she was sure that was what would happen. At least in the short term. Mrs Walton was delighted with her new-found grandson, but Tammy didn't think *she* would ever be forgiven for the death of Jake's father. But if she explained this to Ben, he would attempt to talk her round.

So she said simply. 'It's the wrong time for both of us, Ben.'

She sensed his disappointment as, without a word, he set the car in motion and drove to his aunt's home.

Tammy rushed into the house the moment they arrived and, seeing Mrs Walton in the kitchen, asked, 'Where's Jake?'

'He's in the garden.'

Ben followed and grasped her arm before she reached the door into the garden. 'What's the hurry? He's fine.'

'How do you know? You're not his mother.'

She heard Ben's gasp of dismay as she rushed over to the boy.

Jake was happily engrossed with a box of buttons and two disposable cups, his face smeared with the remains of chocolate cake.

'Hello, Mum.' He looked up and, smiling at her, said, 'Are we going home now?'

'I think that's a good idea.' A very good idea. It was the opportunity she needed to escape.

'It's getting late, Ben. I need to get Jake home to bed.'

Mrs Walton offered her refreshment but she refused and made her apologies.

Promising to visit again, she took Jake's hand and said, 'Thank Mrs Walton for looking after you so well.'

He mumbled his thanks, then she turned to Ben. 'I'm sorry to drag you away.'

Following them to the car, Mrs Walton said, 'Thank you so much for bringing Jake, Tammy. And please, please, come again soon.'

Tammy nodded and smiled.

'Was that my fault you decided to leave so abruptly?' Ben demanded as they set off for home.

'Jake needs to get to bed. You know he was pulled down by that bug—'

'But he was fit enough for you to go to work.' He shook his head. 'I think you need to get your priorities sorted, Tam.'

'I think I have,' she told him coldly. 'Jake's my number-one priority and I'm taking him home.'

'My aunt thinks you were cross about the chocolate cake. I could see she was upset.'

'You don't understand.'

He shrugged. 'We can't talk about this now.' Over his shoulder he nodded towards Jake in the back.

He didn't understand, Tammy told herself. He wasn't Jake's father so Jake wasn't his responsibility. He would never feel like she did about her son's welfare.

Sure, Ben liked spending time with the boy, but if he had children of his own, whether it was with her or anyone else, Jake would be the loser. They'd been thrown together by a series of coincidences and she had felt sorry for him because of the way Deanna had treated him. But neither of these was a reason for entering into another relationship. She'd made one mistake with his cousin and certainly wasn't going to repeat it, however attracted to Ben she might be.

As they drew up to their door, Ben said, 'While you see to *your* son, I'll go back and check that my aunt's OK.'

Tammy nodded, left the car and unlocked the front door so that he could deposit the still sleeping Jake inside the house.

The child woke up as they entered the hall and Ben placed him on the bottom stair and left.

'Sit there a moment, darling.' Aware that she had hurt

Ben, she went out to thank him for the lift home, but all she could see were his taillights disappearing.

When she came back Jake had toppled sideways and his head was resting on the second stair.

'Where's Ben?' he muttered sleepily.

'Gone back to see Mrs Walton.' She placed an arm around his shoulders. 'Come on. Let's get you into your pyjamas and to bed.'

'Why didn't he stay?'

'Mrs Walton needed him and then he has his own home to go to.' If you could call his room in the residency a home. 'Now. Would you like a drink or something to eat?'

Jake stuck his bottom lip out. 'Want Ben to read to me.'

'He can't.'

'Why?'

'He's busy. Come on upstairs, Jake.' She tried to move him.

'I want Ben,' he muttered sleepily.

'We can't always have everything we want, love.'

'Will we see him tomorrow?'

'I don't think so.'

Jake sat back down stubbornly on the bottom step. 'Not fair.'

'Come on, Jake. You'll be more comfortable in bed.' Eventually Tammy persuaded him to let her carry him up and then she read to him herself. That done, she felt physically and emotionally drained, so she went downstairs and settled back in her armchair with a glass of wine. Breathing deeply, she closed her eyes and within a very short time she was sound asleep.

CHAPTER NINE

MRS WALTON was fine and persuaded Ben to stay and eat the sandwiches she had prepared for afternoon tea.

After they had talked over and over the events of the afternoon, he took his leave. He needed to see Tammy and talk to her. Her abrupt departure had made him realise he'd made a complete hash of things—again. If only he'd been patient, the afternoon might have ended very differently. As it was, he loved her so much that he couldn't resist trying to comfort her when she was upset, but it had been the wrong time. Jake's well-being had been the most important thing to her at that moment and he should have realised it instead of storming off in a huff as he had done. Before he went back to the hospital, he had to try to put things right between them.

As he turned the next corner he saw Lauren limping in the direction of the house and cursed inwardly. He'd hoped she'd be out. If she hung around, as she had done a couple of days before, there was no way he was going to be able to tell Tammy how he really felt.

He decided he couldn't drive past her, especially having seen she was limping, so he stopped and offered her a lift the rest of the way.

'Thank you,' she sighed as she sank gratefully into the passenger seat. 'My feet are giving me hell.'

'I could see that. What's the problem?'

'New shoes.'

His hopes lifted slightly. 'I thought this was early for you. You're just home to change?'

'I'm going home, full stop. As Tammy and Jake were

out for the day I caught the train to London to go shopping with friends.'

'Doesn't look as if you bought much.'

She shook her head. 'The shops were crowded so we did more chattering than buying.'

He pulled the car to a stop in front of Tammy's house. There was no point in going in now, but perhaps he could persuade Tammy to come out for a drink.

He walked round to open the door for Lauren. 'If you're not going out again this evening…'

'With these feet? You've got to be joking.'

'In that case, would you mind if Tammy comes out for a quick drink?'

Watching her closely, he held his breath in anticipation. 'Not—'

Ben never heard the remainder of her reply as something struck him between his shoulder blades, knocking him completely off balance.

The last thing he heard was Lauren's scream as a male voice shouted viciously, 'That'll teach him. Trying to muscle in on my girlfriend as well as get me in trouble with the law.'

The scream woke Tammy with a start and she rushed to the front door. As she pulled it open to see if somebody needed help, she heard Lauren shout, 'You stupid fool, Marcus. He gave me a lift home. That's all.'

As Tammy started down the drive she was met by a dishevelled Lauren. 'It's Ben, he's hurt,' she blurted out breathlessly. 'Marcus has gone mad. He caught him unawares,' she gasped, 'from behind. I think Ben hit his head.'

Tammy turned and grabbed her medical bag. 'Get the police, Lauren. And an ambulance. I'll go and see what's happening.'

She raced back down the path and recognised the man standing over Ben as Lauren's ex-boyfriend. In the sternest voice she could muster, she ordered, 'Leave him alone.'

'I didn't mean to hurt him—not like that. Just teach him a lesson.'

She tried to push him away from Ben's side, but he was too strong for her.

He turned unsteadily and staggered against her, his head cracking against Tammy's harder than she would have believed possible. Shocked, she sank to one knee, rubbing her head.

'Oh, hell, I didn't mean to do that either.' He was slurring his words and Tammy guessed he'd been drinking, and heavily at that.

Lauren reappeared at that moment and Tammy was relieved that her shrieked 'What the hell have you done to her, Marcus?' made him turn his attention from her.

Shakily she climbed to her feet and groggily moved to where Ben was lying motionless.

'Ben. It's me, Tammy.' She knelt down at his side and, shaking him gently, repeated his name, but there was no response. She checked his pulse and that he was breathing and then did a rapid check for other injuries. Not finding any sign of bleeding, she moved his limbs in preparation for turning him into a safe position for an unconscious patient.

Before she could do so his eyes flickered open.

'Hello, Ben. You're doing fine, but just lie still for me.' She could hear the sound of sirens coming closer and looked up to see Marcus running off down the road.

'Should I go after him?' Lauren was hovering reluctantly.

'No. Leave him.'

'Is—is he alive?' Lauren's face was white as she looked down at Ben, whose eyes were closed again.

'Yes, he's fine.' Tammy wished she felt as confident as she was trying to sound. 'It sounds like the ambulance will be here soon, so could you go and check Jake for me? Then stay indoors with him.'

Lauren nodded and moved away slowly, casting anxious glances back at the scene.

'Ben, love. Do you hurt anywhere?'

He opened one eye and experimentally touched his head, wincing as he tried to move.

She grasped his hands gently. 'Best if you keep still until we get you properly checked out, but as far as I can tell there's no serious damage.'

'Wh-what happened?'

'Marcus knocked you down. Lauren thinks you hit your head.'

'Marcus?'

'Lauren's ex-boyfriend. The police will go after him. They're here now.'

As she spoke a police car and ambulance arrived. The paramedics jumped out and Tammy told them what had happened. 'We're both doctors at Marton General. I've checked him over.'

As one paramedic did the same, she recited her findings.

'We'll take him to Marton Casualty—but we'll check him first.' A stretcher was already wheeled into place. 'Do you want to come with him?'

She clambered to her feet. 'I'd better see if my nanny's all right. She saw what happened and is pretty shocked.'

'We'll connect him to the monitors before we move off.'

'See you later, Ben. Take care.' Tammy kissed his cheek and as he was lifted into the back of the ambulance she turned to walk towards the house where a policeman was talking to Lauren at the front door, but her legs suddenly refused to support her. The second policeman caught her. 'Are you injured?'

'I don't think so. Just…' Her voice trailed off.

'The girl says you were hit on the side of the head by her boyfriend's head and she is upset because it's all her fault. You'd better be checked out as well.'

His words made Tammy aware that there was no way she could leave Jake in the care of someone in such a state. 'I can't go. Lauren needs me, and anyway he might come back. I'll be OK.'

'We'll call up a policewoman to stay with her.'

'My parents will come over if I can ring them, but I do need to stay with Lauren until they arrive. In case my son wakes up.' Jake had been through quite enough for one weekend without waking up to find a policewoman looking after him.

By this time the flashing lights had attracted several neighbours to the scene. One handed her a mobile phone. 'Don't worry, sir. We'll contact them if she gives us the number.' He turned to Tammy. 'You go in the ambulance now.'

She shook her head. 'I'm not going until I see Lauren's all right.'

Shrugging, the policeman waved the ambulance away and then helped Tammy indoors.

She settled on the chair beside Lauren and put her arm around the girl while her parents were contacted. After a brief explanation they agreed to come straight over.

Tears were streaming down the younger woman's cheeks. 'I'm sorry. So sorry. I'd no idea…' Her voice tailed off as the policemen started comparing notes.

'You knew this chap who hit him?' he asked Lauren.

'He was my boyfriend until last week.'

'Is that when you started dating the doctor?'

'No. No. He was Tammy, Dr Penrose's boyfriend. He just gave me a lift from the end of the road.'

As they all turned to look at her, Tammy shook her head.
'I work with him. That's all.'

'You're saying neither of you were in a relationship with him?'

'No,' they chorused.

'So why was he coming here?'

'He's recently discovered he's related to Jake, my son.'

Lauren gasped. 'Related? Really? How—? I'd no idea.'

'Mrs Penrose, how old is your son?'

'Four.'

The two police officers exchanged glances. 'And he's only just found that out?'

She nodded and ran a hand over her forehead. 'It's a long story. Do you think it could wait? I'd like to go and check on my son.'

Jake was still sound asleep, so Tammy moved into her own bedroom to give herself some peace to think. She longed to be with Ben, to see how he was. He had clearly had a bad knock on the head and she knew how dangerous those could be. 'Please, God,' she muttered, 'don't let him die. I couldn't bear to lose him.'

The same thought had crept insidiously into her mind when she'd seen him lying on the pavement. She'd told the police they weren't in a relationship but, oh, how she wished they were. Ben had obviously wanted that, but she hadn't trusted him or his motives and yet, now he was in danger, she knew she really did love him.

She blinked back tears that refused to be dammed behind her eyes any longer. Was she too late? Lauren had denied that she and Ben had dated, but why had Marcus been so incensed? Why had he hit Ben? What did he know that she didn't?

Tammy heard her parents arrive and thrust her sudden fears to the back of her mind. It was all too much. She'd have to try and work it out later. Her brain wasn't functioning on all cylinders at the moment.

When she'd come downstairs, her mother rushed to hug her. 'Are you all right, love?'

The embrace released a fresh flow of tears, so all Tammy could do was nod.

'I need to go to the hospital. Can you stay with Lauren and Jake? Perhaps Dad would take me.'

'Are you hurt?'

'No. I—'

'She had a blow on the head and needs to be checked over,' the older policeman told her.

'Is the man in custody?'

'Not yet. But this young lady has told us where he lives.'

'Why did he do it?'

'That's something we'll have to discover when we find him.'

And something I need to know, Tammy thought. Soon.

'If you go to the hospital now, Dr Penrose, we'll continue these questions tomorrow.'

'What about Marcus?'

'We'll arrest him when we find him, never fear. Keep your doors locked until we do.'

'Could you drop me at the hospital, Dad, and then come straight back to be with Mum? I'll call you when I want to come home or, better still, I'll get a taxi.'

Her mother looked relieved. 'Of course Dad'll take you to get yourself checked out, love. And we'll stay as long as we're needed. Lauren and I are just going to have a cup of coffee.'

Tammy insisted on going into the hospital alone. 'I'm fine now, Dad. I've got my mobile and I'll ring you.'

'If you're sure you'll be all right?'

'Of course I will, and I'll be happier knowing you're with Mum and Lauren.'

He kissed her before she got out of the car. 'After you've seen Ben, make sure they take a look at you. Promise. And ring me when you want to come home—don't wait for a taxi.'

She nodded and tears threatened as he put the car in gear and drove away. A man of few words was her dad, but so perceptive. He knew perfectly well she was here for one reason only and that was to see Ben.

She made her way to the accident and emergency department and went in search of the nurse in charge.

When she couldn't find her she told the evening receptionist who she was and asked if Helen Smith was on duty.

'She's in Resus. Dr Davey's had an accident and everybody's running around like headless chickens.'

Tammy nodded. 'I'll wait in her office.'

She didn't. She made her way to Resus and popped her head round the door and mouthed, 'How is he?'

Helen beckoned her in.

'Improving, but still a little confused. The neuro team think it's probably just concussion but we're waiting for X-rays. I gather it happened outside your house?'

Tammy heard the interest in her voice and ignored it. 'Yes. He'd given my nanny a lift home.'

'Your nanny?' She looked disappointed and not a little suspicious. 'Was she hurt?'

Tammy shook her head. There was no way now she was going to admit she'd been the one hit. That really would fuel the speculation!

Jeff Reid, the casualty officer on duty, came over to speak to Helen and she told him who Tammy was. He nodded a greeting. 'We're going to admit Dr Davey so that we can keep a close eye on him overnight. He's badly concussed and there is a faint suspicion of a hairline fracture. At the moment he can't remember what happened either before or since.'

Tammy nodded. 'By all accounts, his head hit the pavement quite heavily. I don't think he sustained any other injuries.'

'We've checked him over and there's some nice bruises developing but nothing to indicate serious damage, and his obs are stable at the moment. How did you hear about it?'

'He was with my nanny at the time.'

Unlike Helen, he accepted her explanation. 'Do you want to go with him?'

She nodded and to allay further any hospital gossip she said, 'I'll stay for a short time then I can reassure Lauren about his condition. I'll wait outside while you get him organised.'

In the waiting area one of the two police officers who'd been at the house was talking to the house officer.

When he saw Tammy, he came across and told her, 'You'll be pleased to know, Dr Penrose, that Mr Cusack is in custody. One of our colleagues found him under the influence on the riverbank.'

'Mr Cusack—oh, you mean Marcus.' She'd never known his surname.

Ben's trolley emerged from the resus room at that moment so she walked over to it and smiled down at him. 'Hi.'

She didn't hear his reply because the police officer called, 'Have the doctors checked you over, Dr Penrose?'

'No need. I'm fine.'

Ben squinted up at her. 'I've always thought so. What happened to you, then?'

'I banged my head.'

He frowned and tried to raise his head from the trolley.

'Calm down, Ben. No damage done.'

'If you're hurt…'

'I'm not.'

The small effort he had made must have been too much

for him so he closed his eyes and said nothing more until he was settled in the HDU.

The staff had put him in a small side room, but as they were busy there was no one available to special him, so Tammy offered to stay. 'I can see you're stretched to the limit.'

The nurse in charge of the night shift accepted gratefully. 'That's great, but don't hesitate to call us if you're worried.'

Ben had drifted off to sleep again and Tammy seated herself beside him, keeping her eye on the monitors and checking his pupils frequently. It was nearly a couple of hours later when she noticed his pulse rate was decreasing and his blood pressure rising. Minimally, to be sure, but rising. She checked his eyes again and convinced herself there was a slight inequality in the size of the pupils. When she spoke to him there was no response, although he did react to her touch.

Aware that she was too close to him to make a decision about his condition, she called the nurse in charge of the unit and showed her the changes on Ben's chart where she had been recording observations.

'I'm not happy about his pupils either.'

After checking his eyes with a flashlight, she said tersely, 'I'll get someone from the neuro team back.'

Within an incredibly short time, another scan was organised which would show what was happening inside his skull.

After popping outside for a breath of fresh air, Tammy returned to the unit to wait for Ben's return. She massaged her temples in an attempt to think clearly and dislodge the clamouring ache. She knew it was nothing more than re-action to everything that had happened, but she felt that if she didn't get some sleep soon her head would burst.

Finding Ben's room still empty and no one about to tell her what was happening, she seated herself in a comfortable chair in the waiting area, intending to ask if she could use the unit's telephone to contact her parents.

She was woken by a hand shaking her arm gently and apparently repeating her name. 'Dr Penrose.'

She blinked herself awake, trying to work out where she was.

It was a nurse she hadn't seen before. 'Dr Davey is back in his room and doing OK. You can see him quickly and then you ought to get off home and sleep properly.' She smiled. 'You've had quite a shock this evening.'

Tammy nodded and asked what the scan had shown. 'Are they going to operate?'

The nurse frowned. 'Operate? Not that I know of. I'll get the house officer to come and explain.'

A little later Neil Goss smiled at her and explained, 'The scan showed that there is some swelling of the brain but I'm glad to say that there is no immediate need of intervention. It would be great, though, if you could stay and continue to monitor his condition.'

She nodded. 'No problem. I'll stay the night.' Hammers in her own head were making her feel quite ill but she didn't want to leave Ben's side until she knew he was improving.

She couldn't keep saying it was for her nanny's benefit, though, or tomorrow they'd start to wonder why Lauren didn't visit. It was difficult when she was not Ben's next of kin and they weren't even in a relationship. She wasn't even sure she had the right, except as his junior doctor, however much she longed now to be something more.

But he was related to her son. Was that a good enough reason? Her son's second cousin—good grief, she'd never given Ben's aunt a thought. What was the matter with her? How could she have forgotten his real next of kin? She was a doctor, for goodness' sake. She should have thought about his family long ago. She ought to ring Mrs Walton right away and let her know. But…it was late at night and she lived alone. And she had already lost her son. What would the news do to her if she thought she might lose Ben?

Tammy grasped the nurse's arm as she was leaving. 'Could I ring and let my parents know what's happening?'

'Sure.' She pointed to the office. 'Come through when you're ready.'

As she dialled, Tammy checked her watch. Five minutes past midnight. No way was she going to disturb Mrs Walton's beauty sleep now. 'Sorry not to have rung before, Dad. You go to bed and I'll get a taxi later.'

'How's Ben?'

She swallowed. 'In good hands, but I'm not happy about his condition so I'd rather stay for a while and see that he's OK. As usual the staff are overstretched.'

'Have they had a look at you?'

'I'm fine, Dad. Honest. How's Lauren?'

'She's sleeping. So's your mother and we haven't heard a peep out of Jake. And don't worry about the morning. We can both take the day off work if necessary.'

'Thanks, Dad. I hadn't even thought about tomorrow— or today I suppose it is. I've got to be on duty by eight.' And on call tomorrow night, she thought regretfully as she replaced the receiver. She'd have to think about that nearer the time. Ben was the one she needed to think about now.

She felt much better for her nap and was able to stay awake and do observations every quarter of an hour until the day shift came on duty. Ben stirred occasionally but Tammy tried to disturb him as little as possible.

After taking the hand-over report, the nurse in charge came in to see them both. 'Hi, I don't think we've met. I'm Judy Dunn.'

Tammy smiled in acknowledgement and explained what was happening with Ben.

'I'm told you've done sterling work here overnight but

that you're on duty today, so I'll take over now. I've put a tray of tea in the relatives' waiting area so that you can have a rest before you start.' She smiled. 'You look as if you need it.'

'I'll be OK. At least I've not been rushing around like I do when I'm on call. I'll have to go soon, though, as Mike Rolf does a ward round this morning and Ben won't be there.'

Despite that, after drinking half a cup of tea, she drifted off to sleep again and Judy didn't wake her but rang the sister on Clarke Ward.

The first thing she heard was Mike's voice. 'Tammy, Ben's fine and I've arranged for locum cover. I want you to go home now and get some sleep.'

Tammy looked at him with wild eyes, 'I'm sorry.' She checked her watch and groaned. 'I'd no idea it was that time. I'm so sorry.' She leapt to her feet.

He gently pushed her back down into the chair. 'You're not working today, Tammy. First I want the neuro bods to check you over, then you're going home. You can see Ben first if you like, but then you do as I say. Right?'

She swallowed hard to try and prevent the tears that had sprung to her eyes spilling over.

'I'm all right.'

'Maybe, but we need to have it confirmed. I can't manage without both of you.'

'Then I'll stay.'

'Not today, you won't. I'll expect you back on duty tomorrow morning, unless the neuro people say differently.'

She could see it was useless arguing and, with her tears refusing to be contained, she thanked him.

He helped her to her feet. 'Neil Goss is on his way here to take a look at you, then, while you see Ben, I'll contact Neil and if he's happy you get off home. Where's your car?'

'At home, but I'm sure my father will collect me.' Then, realising it was Monday and she hadn't rung them since late the previous night, she clapped a hand to her mouth. 'I must ring and see what's happening there.' She took out her mobile and was about to make her way outside when Mike said, 'Use the office phone. I don't want you escaping.'

She smiled. 'All I did was knock heads with Ben's attacker—probably a bruise there but nothing more.'

He nodded. 'Maybe, but Ben refuses to rest easy until you've been checked over.'

'How…?' She frowned and shook her head as a feeling of warmth spread right through her body. Someone must have told him she'd had a knock and hadn't seen a doctor. As if he didn't have enough problems of his own to cope with.

'OK.' She grinned. 'I'll do what I'm told this time.'

When she'd eventually seen Neil and had been pronounced fit and well, she made her way back to Ben's room.

He was awake and greeted her with a smile. 'I hear you're all right.'

She shook her head in amazement. 'You know everything before I do. Have you got me bugged?'

He laughed. 'No. Just a good grapevine.'

'Who told you?'

'Neil asked Judy Dunn to let me know.'

'But how did you know I'd had a bang and hadn't been seen by anyone?'

'I heard the policeman say so.'

'I thought you couldn't remember anything that happened.'

'That was last night. I've slept since then and my memory's gradually returning. The important bits first.' He eyed her mischievously. 'I seem to remember you calling me "love" when I was lying stunned on the pavement.'

'I was trying to get a response from you. That was all.'

'Is that why you kissed me when you had to leave me?'

'I was worried about you. Like I am about you now.'

Ben looked up at her and grinned. 'I do hope that'll be the first of many. Perhaps we could try again when I get to my room. They've said I can leave here as long as I take it easy.'

'You're not going to your room in the residency?'

'I'm not staying here.'

'You can't go to that cell on your own. Who'll check on you there?'

He shrugged. 'I know what to watch for.'

'But if you become drowsy you may not realise—'

'Stop worrying. I'll be fine.'

'You will not. Why don't you go and stay with your aunt?'

'She would make such a fuss and be so worried.' He paused and then said, 'I take it she wasn't told I'm in here?'

Tammy shook her head. 'It was too late last night when I thought of it.'

'Thank goodness for that.'

'Well, there's no way you are going to be left on your own. You'd better come home with me. At least for the night. I'll move Jake in with me and *I'll* keep an eye on you.'

'I can't let you to do that. I don't want to upset Jake.'

'Jake would like nothing better—he wanted you and no one but you to read to him last night when we got home.'

He lifted an eyebrow wryly. 'Glad to know I'm still popular with at least one member of the family?' He delivered the words as a query but Tammy didn't take the hint.

'I'm only doing this because you're a good registrar and I wouldn't want any patient to go home alone with concussion,' she told him severely. 'And I promise I won't let Jake pester you too much.'

He chuckled. 'I sure do appreciate your concern, ma'am, and I'd like to take you up on your offer for the night. I'll be returning to work after that.'

'We'll see about that when the time comes. I don't have my car here so I'll go and ring my father and ask him to collect us.'

Tammy also asked her mother if she would start moving Jake's bits and pieces into her own room and make up the spare bed for Ben.

'Will Jake sleep with you in the double bed or do you want his bed moved as well?'

'I'll help move the bed when I get home.'

'Good job it's a large room,' her mother commented dryly.

'Is Jake OK?'

'He's fine, love. Missing you, so Lauren's taken him out to the swings and is going on to visit a friend. They haven't been gone long.'

'Probably a good thing if Ben can settle in before Jake starts pestering him. See you soon, Mum.'

She went back to Ben's room where she found him already dressed in the clothes he'd been wearing the day before.

'I'd like to collect a few clean clothes from my room, if that's OK.'

She nodded. 'We'll do that now. Dad'll be here in about twenty minutes.'

When they got to his room he turned with surprising agility and, pulling her to him, unerringly placed his lips on hers.

'Hey, Ben Davey.' She smiled up into his eyes. 'You're supposed to be taking it easy and Dad'll be here in a minute. Get packing.'

She watched from the corridor while he threw a few shirts and socks into a small holdall and collected some toiletries.

'Right. I think that's all.'

She insisted on taking the bag from him and held his arm as they walked to the main entrance to await their transport. She introduced him to her father when he arrived and was pleased to see they appeared to like one another on sight.

When they got to Tammy's house she saw the same could be said for her mother. Tammy took Ben's bag upstairs and showed him the room. 'Do you want to have a rest now?'

He gave her a very straight look. 'I'm not an invalid and I hate all the trouble I'm causing.' He peered round the door of the main bedroom where Jake's bed was already alongside her own. 'And there's not really enough room in there for his bed, is there?'

'It'll be fine.'

'I could have shared your room—after all, it won't be the first night we've spent together, will it?'

She heard her mother gasp behind them and Tammy wondered if Ben was hallucinating, then she saw the quick flicker of an eyelid as he winked at her and whispered, 'I mean, you never left my side for a moment last night, did you?'

CHAPTER TEN

IT TOOK a full five minutes of explanation before Tammy managed to convince her mother that Ben really had only been joking. Not that she should need to explain when she was a qualified doctor with a four-year-old son, but her mother and father had done so much for her during her training and since Jake had been born that she couldn't bear the thought of such a silly thing upsetting them.

Despite her efforts, when Ben joined them in the kitchen, her mother clearly found it difficult to be as friendly as she had been on his arrival.

Eventually she said, 'I think it will be best if your dad and I go home now, Tammy. Lauren and Jake will be back soon and I'm sure Dr Davey will be better with fewer people around.'

Tammy agreed it would probably be a good idea. 'Thanks, Mum, both of you, for what you've done. And for taking the day off work. I don't know what I'd have done without you.'

Ben grasped her hand and shook it warmly. 'I want to thank you for what you've done for Tam as well, Mrs Penrose. Not just today either. I know you're a terrific support to her in her career. And, please, call me Ben.'

'Yes, well…' Mary Penrose giggled.

He gave her a scintillating smile. 'Your daughter is a great doctor and it would be our loss if she couldn't work.'

Tammy hid a grin as she watched the effect of his flattery on her mother.

But Ben hadn't finished. He turned to her father. 'I would be very worried if she hadn't been checked over at the

175

hospital so, thank you, sir, for taking her and providing transport for us this morning.'

He, too, fell under the spell of Ben's charm at that point and mumbled, 'No problem. And I do hope you soon feel better.'

'I'm fine. It's only the doctor in Tam fussing that made me agree to come here for the night so that she could keep an eye on me. Then I intend getting back to work.'

'Only if I consider you fit,' Tammy told him firmly.

When her parents had collected their bits and pieces together and had left, asking her to give Jake a cuddle from them, Tammy led the way back into the sitting room.

'What on earth made you say such an outrageous thing? Didn't you hear Mum come up behind us?'

He grinned. 'Outrageous? I don't think so. Tammy, I—'

'Tammy now, is it? And don't think I didn't notice you calling me Tam a few moments ago!'

'Sorry.' Ben hung his head in mock shame. 'That wasn't intentional, I promise, but that's how I always think of you. Constantly.'

'That bang on your head seems to have knocked the sense out of you.'

He shook his head and moved close enough to place his arms on her shoulders, intending to reinforce his message with his steady gaze. 'I mean it, Tammy. I do think about you all the time.'

For a second her eyes held his and then she caught her breath sharply and demanded, 'Me and who else?'

He frowned. 'What? Who do you mean?'

'You ask me that when Marcus apparently thought Lauren had finished with him in favour of you. How do I know that isn't the truth? You certainly made a big impression on her the other evening.'

'Tammy,' he reproached her, 'I would have thought you knew me better than that by now. That young lady is far too immature for my tastes, but—and it's a big but...' He paused, making Tammy wait for the denouement, aware by his grin that he was teasing her. 'She scares the hell out of me, far, far too nubile.'

'And I'm not? Thanks for the compliment.' She sank back into her seat.

'Tammy, you have a serene sexual maturity that defies description and I love it.' He moved closer again and nibbled gently at her ear before saying, 'It was one of the things that first attracted me to you.'

His hot breath on her cheek started to flood her body with sensations that she knew would soon overwhelm her and prevent her discovering the truth. She pulled away from him again and swung round to face him. 'So what were you doing with Lauren outside my house yesterday evening?'

The look of horrified amazement on his face almost convinced her before he spoke. 'I wasn't doing anything with her. I was coming to see you. But when I saw her limping along the road, what else could I do but offer her a lift home? That guy must have been waiting outside for her and assumed she'd been out with me. I never stood a chance—didn't even know what had hit me until I was on the ground.'

'Lauren says he accused you of getting him in trouble as well. What did he mean by that?'

'Mike and I have become increasingly concerned about the number of chest problems occurring amongst the employees of Blacktrees Chemicals. I mentioned as much to one of the inspectors who visited Percy Good following the explosion and they've been looking into it.'

She shook her head thoughtfully and allowed herself to relax back into the arm that he had again placed firmly round her shoulders. 'You're not pressing charges against him?'

Ben pulled her gently closer and said, 'I don't think it'll be necessary. It was the drink talking and who can blame him for fighting for such a lovely girl? As to the conditions at the chemical plant, I'd rather work with him to get conditions right for the men than against him.'

His explanations made her feel much happier and she turned to him, a lazy smile playing around her lips. 'You can stop saying that about other girls if you want to stay here for even one night. Concussion or no.'

He hugged, then kissed her, then hugged her even more tightly. 'Wonderful, Tammy. You're jealous. That must mean—'

'It means I'm not a saint but a human being, and I don't want to be put on a pedestal!'

He laughed. 'You should get fired up more often. I thought there must be a temper that went along with that red hair, but you certainly keep it well hidden. Pity really. You look so beautiful when aroused.' He kissed her cheek then his lips met hers with a tender certainty. Her breathing quickened and, swept up in a swirling mist of desire, she surrendered to the gentle plundering of her mouth which left her unable to do anything but respond.

When he finally released her lips and raised his head, he smiled as their eyes met and said, 'Wowee! You're not a saint, are you?'

She was about to indignantly protest when he hugged her even more tightly to his chest and murmured, 'I do love you so much, Tamsin Penrose.'

When she didn't speak he asked, 'Do you love me even just a little?'

Tammy certainly wanted him, but was that the same thing? She shook her head to try and clear it and, after taking a deep breath, said, 'More than just a little, Ben, but whether it's enough to overcome the obstacles ahead, I'm still not sure...'

'What obstacles?'

'Jazz, Jake, your aunt, the fact that I need to concentrate on my exams…'

'If we love one another we can overcome all those. Don't—'

'If the time was right, but I'm not sure it is. I think we should take it slowly, Ben, especially after the emotions raised by your accident.' She recalled her fear that she'd been about to lose him when she'd seen him lying on the pavement, and shuddered. 'I was frightened you were going to die.'

'I wouldn't leave you, Tam, not when I've just found you.' His arms encircled her, cradling her closely to his chest.

They were silent for a few moments, then Ben asked, 'What are you thinking about?'

'Marcus.'

'Marcus?' The name exploded from his lips.

'Is he really in trouble because of the working conditions at the chemical factory?'

'Is this important? I want to talk about us.'

'It is really. I'm trying to understand why he reacted so violently.'

He sighed deeply. 'I don't think any action has been taken against the company or any individual up to now. But obviously something's been said by the health and safety inspector and that must have been the last straw when he realised who it was, bringing his ex-girlfriend home. I think Blacktrees have tried to get it right, but the doctors they employed never had enough time. They've had a succession of them, but it has all been very haphazard. They need to employ someone who knows what they're doing and I'm sure, like me, the inspectors would rather work with them, including Marcus, to get it right though there may still be other repercussions.'

Tammy ran a finger lightly down his cheek. 'You really care about people, don't you?'

'Don't all doctors?'

'Debatable. Could you say that of Peter?'

He uttered a mirthless snort.

'I gather you're not his number-one fan.'

'He was partly instrumental in my break-up with Deanna.'

Tammy frowned. 'She was a doctor?'

'No. A high-flying businesswoman who went across to Europe quite frequently. Funnily enough, Peter was at the same hospital then and as she wanted me to go with her sometimes she demanded to know why I couldn't have as much time off as he did.

'If I have one fault, it's that I can be impetuous. I really hoped that my medical training had cured me of it. It seems obviously not when it comes to affairs of the heart. When Deanna told me she wasn't prepared to take a break in her career to have our children, I thought I'd blown my chance of happiness when I rashly broke off our relationship, but when I met you I knew it had been the right thing. I didn't know what love was until you came along.

'And that's why, darling, I'm not going to waste another moment. Tamsin Penrose, I love you, have done since the first day we met and will do for the rest of our lives. So tell me you'll marry me, please?'

When Tammy didn't reply immediately but pulled out of his arms with a thoughtful expression, he begged. 'Say you will, please. And put me out of my misery.'

'Ben, it's not twenty-four hours since you had a serious bang in the head. I think this should wait.'

'I don't want to wait.' His cry was anguished. 'I love you, Tam. This is nothing to do with my head injury. I was on my way to ask you this last night—'

'Aren't you forgetting about Jake?'

'How could I? He's a lovely lad and I'll be proud to call him "son." And every day we're not living together as a family, we're all missing out.'

'But, Ben, I'm a doctor. I'm working for exams at the moment. I couldn't just give it all up any more than Deanna could.'

'I wouldn't expect you to, but if I could support you both, you'd want to work fewer hours so you can spend time with Jake, wouldn't you?'

'Well, yes. For Jake's sake I've already made up my mind to look for a general practice job share, but—'

'I'd be the last to ask you to give it up completely. I know what it's meant to you to get this far.'

Before she could say anything he took both her hands in his and said in a serious voice, 'Tammy, it's not surprising that you don't feel able to commit yourself to marrying me. So, before Lauren and Jake return, I want to apologise to you.'

She frowned. 'Apologise? For what?'

'For being too impetuous and trying to rush you. I was completely out of order and that's why I was on my way to see you last night.'

She gave him a dreamy smile. 'I rather enjoyed your advances at the time but I was worried your relationship with your aunt could suffer.'

'You think about everybody before yourself, Tammy. You're too good for me,' he murmured gently. 'I was so proud of you when you told my aunt what a wonderful son she had.'

'I still go hot and cold when I think of the way I've destroyed your memory of him.'

'Tammy, when I suspected who Jake's father was I have to confess I was puzzled by the glowing character reference you gave him that night we went for a meal. Soon, however, having watched you eschew all gossip at the hospital,

I realised you said what you did about James because you wouldn't speak ill of anyone, especially not the dead. You see, I was pretty sure that if James had changed to that extent and was no longer the selfish person I remembered, he'd have gone to see his parents long ago.'

'Like you said, we all have faults.'

'I admire your loyalty Tam, and I'm just grateful, for my aunt's sake, that you don't feel the necessity to tell all and sundry.'

'Don't forget it wouldn't reflect well on my judgement of character, would it?'

'I think your judgement might just have matured, Tam.'

He drew her closer, his hand stroking her hair until her cheek was resting on his chest, then dropped a kiss lightly on the top of her head.

'I love you so much, Tammy, but I'm not surprised that you found it difficult to trust me. Ever since I saw the photograph of James in your album I've been trying to rush you into a relationship. I already knew I wanted to marry you, and when I saw the misery in your face that night, I just wanted to comfort you. But I guess you thought it was because of Jake?'

When she still remained silent, he hugged her to him again and said urgently, 'If you still feel it's too soon, Tam, I'm more than prepared to wait.'

Then she felt him stir and lifted her face to meet his lips with her breathing quickening in anticipation. This time she returned his kiss with a fervour that allowed his tongue to gently tease her lips apart.

When they eventually broke for air, she ran her tongue round her lips to savour the sweet taste of him lingering there.

He smiled down at her and, feeling absurdly happy, she giggled.

He tightened his arms around her again. 'Oh, Tammy. I do love you so much.'

'I don't think I've got the hang of this trust thing even now. When I left your aunt's house yesterday I still couldn't quite believe you loved Jake and me enough not to let us down. I—'

He kissed her, this time long and hard. 'It's an unusual, if not unique situation we've found ourselves in and it's not easy for either of us, but I can assure you that I was attracted to you from the moment we met on your first day. And my feelings for you both have nothing to do with Jake being my relative.'

His lips met hers again with a feather-light touch that left Tammy breathless and wanting more, much more. When his hand moved down to undo the top button of her blouse, she slid down into a more comfortable position and when he did the same and moved closer, the messages his body transmitted left her in no doubt he was speaking the truth.

'I do love you, Ben. Very much indeed. I think I knew from the beginning as well but I could also see the problems. It was only when I saw you lying on the pavement yesterday evening that I knew they didn't matter. It would make me very happy to marry you.'

He held her even more tightly then and, his breathing becoming increasingly urgent and heavy, he whispered suggestively, 'We could use that double bed upstairs while Jake is out with Lauren.'

A door slammed and with a rueful smile Tammy pushed him away and straightened her clothes. 'Too late.'

Jake rushed in, calling, 'Grandma, look at this. I found it…' He stopped and gave an excited whoop. 'You're here, Ben, not Grandma.' He launched himself towards his hero.

Aware that it was taking him a little longer to compose

himself, she fended Jake off. 'Dr Davey has had an accident. We have to be careful and look after him.'

Jake nodded importantly and stepped back. 'I can read you a story.'

'Thank you, Jake,' Ben replied gravely. 'I'd like that.'

Jake ran off to find a book, leaving Lauren to ask after Ben's health.

Explanations over, she asked quietly, 'Would it be all right if I go out for a short time this evening, Tammy?'

'Perfectly all right,' Tammy assured her. 'I'll be staying in to keep an eye on my patient. That's why he's here after all.'

Ben looked at her with a mocking lift of his eyebrows.

They all ate together and then Tammy took Jake up for his bath while Ben rested. He did read Jake one story before Tammy took the boy upstairs again and settled him for the night.

Almost immediately they were disturbed by Lauren bringing Marcus in to apologise to Ben.

In the hall Tammy asked Lauren, 'Is your romance on again?'

'I should say so. I'm very proud of him.'

Tammy frowned. 'Proud?'

'He must love me very much to fight for me, however misguidedly.'

Tammy reported this exchange to Ben some time later.

'We can all do silly things where our hormones are concerned. And talking of hormones...' He leaned over and nibbled at her ear before moving much closer and saying, 'It's a pity your son is in your bedroom.'

'I doubt if he'll wake if we move him to his own room. And he'll be happy to find himself there in the morning.'

'How would you explain it to Lauren?'

'Say he went to the toilet and made his way back to the wrong bed? So you moved into the single one in my room?'

Ben nodded happily. 'I'll have to remember to move in the morning.'

Later, much later, a niggling curiosity made Tammy ask, 'What were you and Marcus talking about?'

'He wanted to know if Mike and I would be willing to help with the health screening programme at Blacktrees Chemicals.'

'You can't fit that in. Not on top of all you do at the hospital.'

'It might just be possible if my house officer is willing to give a hand occasionally. And it would eventually cut our workload at the hospital. Would you be interested, Tammy?'

'I guess so.'

'And perhaps consider a part-time job there in the future. Live near home. No on-call duties. And a grounding in occupational health.'

'Why do I get the idea that I'm being manipulated?'

'I can't imagine.' He grinned. 'What do you think of the idea?'

'Having got this far, I'm not going to abandon my general practice exams.'

'I wouldn't ask you to do that, Tam. It could be useful in the future.'

'And what about when you move on to a consultant's job? If I come with you, they'll be left with no one at the factory again.'

'I'm hoping to stay at this hospital. Mike told me this morning he is moving on to a professorship at his teaching hospital, so I'm going to apply for his job. He's promised to recommend me. And consultants are allowed one session a week away from the hospital, if you remember.'

'You've got it all worked out, haven't you?'

'Not really. It just seems to be my lucky day. Everything is slotting into place like a jigsaw. If Marcus hadn't hit me

you wouldn't have agreed to marry me, and if Mike wasn'
leaving I wouldn't be able to help Marcus out at the factory
All I need now is to hear that the house purchase can g
ahead.'

Tammy was four months pregnant when the Davey famil
eventually moved into the house in Park Road. 'Than
goodness for more room. It's taken longer than I woul
have believed possible to get these foundations sorted.'

Tammy smiled. 'I should think we could cope with a
least six children here. And having Mum close will mak
life so much easier. Especially when she gives up wor
next year.'

Jake zoomed noisily into the room. 'This house i
wicked. Where will Lauren sleep?'

Ben ruffled his hair. 'When she and Marcus come bac
from their honeymoon, they'll move into their own hom
But Lauren will be there for you on the days Mummy i
working at the factory. What did you do at school today?

'It's wicked. I can read my own books now.' He rushe
upstairs to his own bedroom.

'Wicked! Is that the only word children know thes
days? Why can't they be taught something positive abou
the world—like love and trust and—'

'Wicked is a good word now—it means wonderful, th
best.'

He grasped her round the waist and gently patted he
burgeoning girth. 'In that case, all I can say is I'm gla
we're both so wicked—in every sense of the word.'

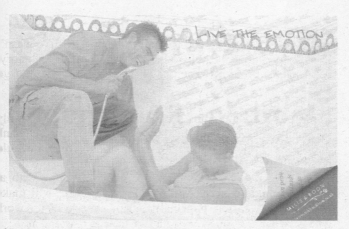

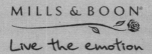

MILLS & BOON®

Live the emotion

Medical Romance™

OUTBACK ENGAGEMENT *by Meredith Webber*

Outback vet Tom Fleming has a problem. After featuring in a magazine as the 'Lonely Country Bachelor' he is surrounded by would-be wives! Merriwee's new doctor, Anna Talbot, is beautiful, blonde and engaged. Perhaps Tom should claim that *he* gave her the ring – having a fake fiancée may end all his woman troubles…

THE PLAYBOY CONSULTANT *by Maggie Kingsley*

Surgeon David Hart puts commitment into work rather than relationships. So he's surprised by his turn-about in feelings when his senior registrar turns out to be Dr Rachel Dunwoody, the woman who walked out on him six years ago! David has some urgent questions. Why did she leave? And, most urgently, how can he get her back?

THE BABY EMERGENCY *by Carol Marinelli*

When Shelly Weaver returned to the children's ward as a single mum, she discovered it was Dr Ross Bodey's first night back too. On discovering her newly single status he'd come back – for her! Suddenly Ross was asking her to change her life for ever – yet Shelly had her son to consider now. Could she make room for them both in her life?

On sale 7th November 2003

Available at most branches of WHSmith, Tesco, Martins, Borders, Eason, Sainsbury's and all good paperback bookshops.

1003/03a

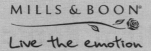

MILLS & BOON®

Live the emotion

Medical Romance™

THE MIDWIFE'S COURAGE *by Lilian Darcy*

Delivering babies all day while knowing she could never have one of her own was hard for midwife Katherine McConnell. Harder still was discovering on her first date with obstetrician Gian Di Luzio that he wanted kids. She had to stop the affair before it even got started. But Gian wanted to be with her above all else...

THE DOCTOR'S CHRISTMAS GIFT
by Jennifer Taylor

Love and family had never been in Dr Catherine Lewis's career plan. But working with Dr Matt Fielding, and playing with his two beautiful daughters, she experiences everything she'd thought she never wanted. As Christmas approaches she must decide if she can she take the risk of a lifetime in Matt's loving arms...

THE SPECIALIST'S SECRET *by Gill Sanderson*

The post of specialist registrar at Dell Owen Hospital means a new life for Dr Alex Storm. He is determined to make an impact on the A&E department – and on Charge Nurse Sam Burns in particular! Sam is certain they could have a magical future – Alex may be secretive about his past but no matter what, Sam is determined that they are going to get through it together!

On sale 7th November 2003

Available at most branches of WHSmith, Tesco, Martins, Borders, Eason, Sainsbury's and all good paperback bookshops.

1003/03b

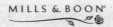

4 FREE

books and a surprise gift!

We would like to take this opportunity to thank you for reading this Mills & Boon® book by offering you the chance to take FOUR more specially selected titles from the Medical Romance™ series absolutely FREE! We're also making this offer to introduce you to the benefits of the Reader Service™—

- ★ FREE home delivery
- ★ FREE gifts and competitions
- ★ FREE monthly Newsletter
- ★ Exclusive Reader Service discount
- ★ Books available before they're in the shops

Accepting these FREE books and gift places you under no obligation to buy, you may cancel at any time, even after receiving your free shipment. Simply complete your details below and return the entire page to the address below. *You don't even need a stamp!*

YES! Please send me 4 free Medical Romance books and a surprise gift. I understand that unless you hear from me, I will receive 6 superb new titles every month for just £2.60 each, postage and packing free. I am under no obligation to purchase any books and may cancel my subscription at any time. The free books and gift will be mine to keep in any case.

M3ZEE

Ms/Mrs/Miss/Mr ....Initials....................................
                                                            BLOCK CAPITALS PLEASE

Surname ....

Address ....

....

....Postcode..........................

Send this whole page to:
UK: FREEPOST CN81, Croydon, CR9 3WZ
EIRE: PO Box 4546, Kilcock, County Kildare (stamp required)